Charming

~ Campus Heat Series ~

M.D. Dalrymple

Charming

Copyright 2021 M.D. Dalrymple
ISBN: 9798701818611
Imprint: Independently published

Cover art and formatting by M.D. Dalrymple

This book is a work of fiction. Names, dates, places, and events are products of the author's imagination or used factiously. Any similarity or resemblance to any person living or dead, place, or event is purely coincidental.

Charming

If you love this book, be sure to leave a review! Reviews are life blood for authors, and I appreciate every review I receive!

Love what you read? Want more from Michelle? Go to the website below for three free ebooks, updates, and more in your inbox

https://linktr.ee/mddalrympleauthor

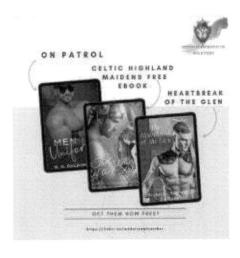

Charming

Table of Contents

Charming	*1*
Chapter One	*7*
Chapter Two	*17*
Chapter Three	*31*
Chapter Four	*39*
Chapter Five	*47*
Chapter Six	*55*
Chapter Seven	*65*
Chapter Eight	*77*
Chapter Nine	*87*
Chapter Ten	*107*
Excerpt from Tempting	*116*
Excerpt from Night Shift	*123*
A Note	*128*
About the Author	*129*
Also by the Author:	*130*

Charming

Chapter One

MARIAH SLAPPED HER phone before it emitted another trilling beep. She had lowered the volume as far as she dared to still be able to wake up for class, but in the dark of night, the ringer still sounded far too loud.

The snoring body next to her grunted and Mariah froze. The apartment was quiet — she even held her breath to make sure she didn't make as sound either. Once the body settled, Mariah lifted the covers and slipped out, as stealthy as a thief.

Charming

And wasn't that what she was doing? Thieving her time away from Derek? Mariah tiptoed to the narrow walk-in closet, and only when the door was secure did she turn on the light.

She blinked in the sudden illumination and released the breath she held as she pulled down the loose tank top, hunter green duster sweater, and dress slacks she had selected the night before. Mariah hated eight a.m. classes and laid out her outfit the night before to cut back on the time it took to get ready.

Once dressed, she shut off the light and slipped to the kitchen to make a small pot of tea, then closed herself in the bathroom to apply a quick layer of makeup.

For a college professor in her late 20s, makeup should have been an area of expertise for Mariah, but having spent much of her late teens and early adult hood with her nose in a book, makeup had remained a mystery to her.

She was fortunate, however, that her lightly tanned skin only needed a quick application of BB cream and makeup that came in iridescent plastic kits, so all she had to do was open one kit and everything else was ready — eyeliner, shadow, mascara, a hint of blush and lip gloss. Her dark brown eyes were easily smoky, so that saved time as well.

Then came the bane of her existence — a fluffy mound of ash-blonde hair that was half wavy, half curly, and always a frizzy mess. Mariah called it her triangle mess. She pulled it into a bun or a banana clip nearly every day and called it good. Her hair was a disaster. She decided on a clip to keep it under control. It was too early to deal with her hair-disaster.

Zipping up her books, she grabbed a to-go cup of tea and her purse waiting by the front door, then peeked in her purse.

Her keys weren't in her purse.

Where the hell are my keys?

She pressed her head against the apartment door and exhaled.

In the bedroom. She had retrieved a book from her car last night before bed and left the keys on her bedside table.

Fuck.

Mariah pulled off her boots and, leaving them by the front door, slipped back into the bedroom which was still dark thanks to the room darkening curtains. She palmed the keys so they wouldn't jingle and made it to the bedroom doorway.

But she missed her count and banged the side of her head against the door jamb.

She held her breath again, sure that the banging woke Derek, but he continued to snore. His late night was paying off in her favor. Rubbing the side of her head, she made it back to the front door, zipped her boots back on, and left.

Escaped was more like it.

Once she was in her car, she fully breathed again.

"I can't live like this," she told herself.

She was an adjunct professor, making enough money to support herself, a feminist who was supposed to be a role model for her young college students, yet she lived with a narcissistic emotional abuser who gaslighted her on a regular basis.

Mariah was not proud.

Charming

Glancing at the clock in her car, she took a sip of her cooling tea and pulled out to the street toward campus.

Mariah's mind drifted as she drove the short trip. Not for the first time, she asked herself what she was doing with Derek. The past few weeks had become a living hell with the man, and she was still letting him sleep over and dictate how to live in her own home.

What the hell is wrong with me?

Why was she letting him do this? She wasn't that type of person. She didn't see herself as that type of person.

In fact, she'd been called a bitch to her face more than once. And she reveled in the term. Why not own it?

What had happened over the past years that made her think she deserved someone like Derek? That was the lone conclusion she could draw — that subconsciously she believed she wasn't deserving of someone better.

Who the hell am I?

But what if her subconscious was telling her something? What if she was only worthy of someone like Derek?

They had met at a bar, of all places.

By God, shouldn't that have been a clue?

Nothing but a meat market, and two of her friends outside campus dragged Mariah there on a Karaoke night. A tallish blond with a decent physique, at least what she could discern from the button down he wore — took the stage and belted out a decent rendition of *Don't Stop Believing*. Mariah had loved it and ended up cheering louder than anyone else in the bar.

The three shots of Fireball hadn't hurt either.

She got his number, made out with him in the parking lot, and called him later in the week.

Most of their dates had been to bars. That should have been her first clue.

But he was so sexy — with light eyes that squinted in a come-hither way that reached into her chest and squeezed her heart.

When was the last time she'd felt that with him? Mariah couldn't recall.

And he had a great job, so he wasn't leeching off her.

Slowly he'd started making requests of her, about her apartment or how she lived. And as much as she hated herself for it, she'd begun to walk on eggshells around him.

And they didn't do anything together. They didn't watch movies and eat popcorn on the couch. They didn't go to any campus events, even though the music festivals were fun. They didn't have long conversations late into the night. They'd eaten out together all of two times. No dates to the park, nothing. Was she overly romantic, or misguided to think that relationships should be more? All they shared was the bar and the bed.

The bar and bed.

He'd been decent enough in bed to start. Giving it his all the first time or two.

Charming

Mariah tapped her fingers on her steering wheel as she waited at a light. She also couldn't recall the last time she came when he was pumping into her. Lately, she'd begun to push him away, using the old "I have a headache" line.

Yeah. Something needed to be done.

She was done.

"Coach! Coach! Wait up!"

Cole Garcia hung his head. Tannis Reyes was a great baller, had a fast ball that was the envy of all the other players in their division, and couldn't pass a class if his life depended on it. He was going to lose his small scholarship if he didn't watch it.

Mount Laguna College wasn't a big state school with a huge athletic presence, but their baseball program was the best in their division, and they recruited kids from high school who weren't quite ready for the bigger colleges and universities. The campus was tucked into a shady Southern California valley, a Division III school with amazing nursing and video tech degree programs, in addition to accomplished sports teams for a college of its size. Coach Garcia was the head baseball coach, and between practices, games, academics, and the petty drama of his player's lives, he sometimes wished he'd gone into the family plumbing business.

"Hey, Tannis! What do you need?"

Charming

Cole wasn't running late, yet — he didn't need to be on campus until closer to noon, but on Tuesdays he had the athletics meeting at eight a.m. sharp. If Tannis had some issue and wanted to talk for hours, that would change.

"Just a quick question, Coach. You said practice was going to end early today? How early, do you know?"

Cole rolled his eyes. Like he was a clock with a perfect schedule.

"I have a late meeting, so we'll be done by four. Four-thirty at the latest."

A bright smile split his pitcher's face.

"Great!"

Cole couldn't help the smile that tugged at his cheeks as well. The kid was bursting with personality.

"What? You got a hot date?" Cole teased.

Tannis fully grinned but shook his head.

"Naw. I got a paper due for Prof Lenski, and I promised her I'd go to the tutor for help."

Cole nodded at Tannis, impressed. Perhaps college was having a positive effect on the man.

"Good for you! Way to take control of your academics."

Tannis's smile faltered. "Not really. She just said if I don't get the extra credit with the tutor, I won't pass. I gotta get a C so I can keep playing. Right?"

Cole agreed. "Right. Still, good for you."

Tannis shot Coach Garcia with his index finger. "Gotcha. See you later, Coach."

His first-string pitcher jogged across the grassy knoll up the side of the humanities building, and Cole studied him as

13

he left. With his sandy brown hair, blue eyes, dusky skin, great baseball skills, and personality for days, Tannis had everything going for him. If he could just get his grades up. Cole was walking the same direction as Tannis, but he had to veer left for the fields and his meeting at the athletics office.

He was passing by cars that managed to park closer than he had when he heard a car door slam and a voice growl, "dammit" under her breath.

Cole peered past a sedan to find the very same, curly haired professor he'd just discussed with Tannis.

"Professor Lenski? Is that you? Do you need help with something?"

Her head popped up like a meerkat from its burrow, and Cole had to physically bite the inside of his cheek not to laugh. Her eyes squinted, trying to place him, then widened.

"What? Oh, hello, Coach Garcia. No, I think, I'm just . . ."

Something dropped to the ground, a heavy text maybe, and she said *dammit* under her breath again. Probably louder than she intended. This time he did smile.

"Here, let me help you."

Cole came around to where she stood in a striking, sweeping sweater that flattered her earthy coloring perfectly. He had seen the professor before — when a player had a professor, Cole tried to at least recognize that instructor. But how did he miss how stunning she was? Not only that, Cole also marveled at her state of dress. He wore blue and white MLC hoodie pullover and sweatpants. That was all he could manage before eight a.m. and coffee.

"Thanks. I was trying to make room in my bag for these papers, but then the books won't fit . . ."

Cole lifted the text from the ground and, in a fluid movement of his hands, grabbed the other books she held.

"Here, I have a few minutes. The Cortez humanities building is right there. How about I walk you to class?"

He didn't realize how that sounded until she crinkled her eyebrows. "Like we're freshmen? You're going to carry my books to class?"

Instead of being embarrassed — Cole didn't shame easily — he widened his smile at the woman.

"Yep. Let's relive a bit of our youth, shall we, Professor Lenski?"

She laughed. Not a timid, weak laugh he expected from a writing professor, but a deep, hearty belly laugh of someone who was sucking all the marrow out of life. As much as he hated to admit it, for all he was the hard coach, he was smitten by that laugh. The way she owned it. *So sexy.* He hoped his face didn't show his surprise.

"It's Mariah. And sure, I could use the extra hands."

She started to walk toward the building and Cole fell into step next to her.

"Cole," he told her. "Please call me Cole."

Charming

Chapter Two

"HEY, HEY. LET'S quiet down. I'll take attendance and then we'll get started for the morning."

Mariah got herself organized and ready for the three-hour Tuesday morning class. It was her sole morning class, thank goodness — she wasn't a morning person — and the students were usually too tired to get very raucous. Tuesday mornings were at least subdued mornings. No chatting students, no loud questions. The worst morning students offered was wearing ear buds during lecture or dozing off before their coffee kicked in.

17

Throughout the class, however, Mariah kept drifting off. While the students worked on their writing projects and peer reviewing, her mind drifted to the well-built, dark-haired baseball coach. Their paths rarely crossed. She didn't spend much time on the athletic fields, and Cole wasn't hanging around the humanities building.

Other than making sure her student-athletes had all the help they needed to maintain a passing grade, she wasn't involved in any sports activities at MLC. But after seeing the tall, dark, and handsome coach, maybe she should. He was like the leading man from a 1930s dramatic film. Only thicker.

Much thicker.

She shook her curls around her face, trying to regain her attention on her class.

And why should she be thinking about Coach Cole Garcia anyway? She was in a relationship, had a boyfriend, didn't she?

After her realization this morning, maybe she didn't. No, she actually didn't. But then, she knew nothing about Cole. He could well be married with kids. Mariah surprised herself with how little she knew about him. Other than a few writing professors in her department, she wasn't friendly with anyone else on campus. Maybe that was her problem. He was someone she didn't know well.

And he was great eye-candy. His ass in those sweats. . . No one said she can't look.

"Prof L? What do we do when we're done with our peer review?" The stunningly beautiful Sabrina asked. Mariah shifted her eyes to the girl. She had the silkiest, straightest black hair Mariah had ever seen. And she was a brilliant writer

18

and strong student. *Some people were born lucky,* she thought. Mariah gave Sabrina Alonto a slight smile.

"Let me change the screen. Here's a list of what you need to do once you have your feedback. And there's fifteen minutes left of class, so if you aren't finished with your peer review, get that done."

Students scrambled to finish, but when Mariah dismissed the class, Sabrina hung behind. A strong but quiet student. Mariah sensed her rather than saw her approach.

"Prof L? Can I ask you a question?"

Her nervous eyes flicked around the room, waiting for everyone to leave. Mariah was used to questions of a private nature. This late in the semester, students had grown to trust her and often came to her with questions outside of writing.

Mariah set her bag on the table so she could focus her attention on the young woman.

"Yes, Sabrina, what can I do for you?"

Sabrina fidgeted for a moment and kept her eyes on her hands. "Um, do you remember how I told you about that guy I dated? The one who didn't seem too stable?"

Mariah stilled. She remembered. Sabrina had come to her when her ex-boyfriend had pushed her. It wasn't a big push and the guy tried to pass it off as a joke, but Mariah encouraged her to study that behavior. Sabrina had dumped him later that week.

The irony of Sabrina's situation wasn't lost on the writing professor who taught irony. Mariah needed to take the same advice she'd given Sabrina and behave with the same strength.

"Yeah. Did something happen?" Mariah's breath froze in her chest. Did the guy turn violent?

"No. But he tried to get back together with me. Even his attempt was pathetic. I just wanted to thank you for helping me through it."

Sabrina raised her eyes. Mariah leaned forward to speak earnestly.

"You deserve the best life possible, Sabrina. Not to be haunted by someone who doesn't deserve you."

Sabrina's face brightened and Mariah was once again struck by how stunning the girl was. If anyone deserved happiness, it was this young woman who seemed to look up to Mariah. Sabrina was an amazing student, a strong writer, and had even asked Mariah for a recommendation to become a writing tutor at the beginning of the semester — a task that Mariah had taken on with glee.

What a horrible role model I am, Mariah lamented to herself, shaking her head slightly. *What am I doing?*

"I hope you are living that life, Prof L. You have really been here for me this semester, and I hope you are living your best life with nothing haunting you. Thanks again. See you next week."

Sabrina lifted her PINK bag and tossed that perfect hair over her shoulder as she left. Mariah's heart ached in her chest.

She stared at the empty desks lined up before her.

Had the girl seen something Mariah tried to keep hidden? Sometimes students were much more astute than she gave them credit for. It didn't matter — Sabrina's words rang true. Mariah needed to take her own advice.

She flicked her eyes to her watch. It wasn't yet noon, and her next class wasn't until two. Derek would be getting out of bed. If she raced home, she could meet him before he left for work, tell him to take his stuff with him when he left, and be done with him.

Sabrina was right. *From the mouths of babes.*

Mariah did deserve better. And now she was going to do something about it.

Derek had finished showering and was dressed for his afternoon shift at the electrical station when Mariah came home for lunch. She braced herself before entering the apartment.

"Hey, Mar. You did good this morning. I slept like a baby."

"That's good."

Her tone was short, clipped, and she set her bag on the kitchen table. If he noticed her discontentment, he didn't seem to register it. Instead, he sipped coffee from her favorite teacup (*of course he would*) and bobbed his blond head to some song only he could hear. His lean frame moved easily around her apartment.

"Derek, we need to talk."

He didn't turn around to face her. "Really, Mar? Not right now. I have to get ready for work. You know that."

"Yeah, I do know that. It's why I want to tell you now. When you leave for work, take all your stuff with you. It's not a lot — it should fit in your backseat easily."

Derek froze, then turned slowly, his handsome face a hard mask. Mariah gritted her teeth, her jaw clenched. She wouldn't let him talk over her or convince her she needed him. Not this time. She was done.

I deserve better, she reminded herself. Mariah chanted it as a mantra in her head.

"No, I'm not. Let's not do anything rash. You know how you are when you make rash decisions."

There he was, gaslighting her again. Like she was somehow mistaken that she wanted to break up.

"Not this time, Derek. I'm done. I don't like tiptoeing around my own apartment. I don't like how you talk to me. I haven't liked a lot for a while now. We're done. Take your stuff and leave."

"Don't talk to me like that. You can't tell me what to do."

His voice held a dangerous edge, but she didn't back down. She pulled her phone from her pocket and dialed two numbers.

"I have 9 and 1 dialed already, Derek," she threatened. "If you don't leave, I'll call the cops and they will make you leave. Now get your stuff and get out."

His green eyes bore into her like a corkscrew, grinding as though he wanted to grind down her will. And in the past, that had worked. This time, it didn't. She wore her words like a shield against him.

"You can't tell me to leave. You're a low-level instructor at a local college. You're nothing," he repeated.

Mariah didn't answer. She just held up her phone with the two numbers already dialed. One additional number and he was done.

She feared he might turn on her. He could easily move from emotional to physical abuse — it happened to women all the time. Still, she glared at him, waiting for him to leave. She stood her ground.

He spun and threw her teacup against the kitchen sink where it exploded into a myriad of shards. She screeched at his burst of violence and covered her eyes. When she dropped her hand and opened her eyes, Derek's face, twisted in anger, filled her view.

"This is a mistake. You can't just come home from a stupid class and kick me out. You'll see. You'll come crawling back to me."

Mariah took a deep breath. *I won.*

"No, I won't."

She leaned against her small kitchen table and watched as Derek stomped into the bedroom. The sounds of slamming drawers and rustling filled the one-bedroom apartment, then Derek appeared, a wad of clothes under his arm.

"Bitch," he spat out.

Mariah didn't even flinch. Pride filled her chest and made her courageous.

Derek slammed the front door as he left, and Mariah's cheek tugged into a side smile.

That felt good. *Too good.* Something she should have done weeks ago. And it took one of her students to help her figure that out.

She took a deep, cleansing breath and went into her kitchen to clean up the shards of her teacup, like she had just cleaned up the shards of her life.

Why had she stayed with Derek as long as she had? Mariah stood at the sink, clutching the frail, broken pieces over the basin. Wispy tendrils of her ash-colored curls escaped her clip and fell on her face, getting trapped by the tears she didn't realize were coursing down her cheeks. Once she gathered all the pieces she could find from the sink, Mariah thew them in the trash and wiped her cheeks with her sleeve. Derek didn't deserve her tears.

She took a deep breath, trying to control her shaking nerves. Class started in just over an hour, and she couldn't go to class looking like she'd spent the day crying her eyes out, even if that was what she was doing.

Mariah pressed her hands against the counter, supporting herself as she hung her head low between her shoulders. *Inhale, count to six. Exhale, count to six.* The yoga breathing she'd learned in her lone yoga class years ago helped in stressful situations like these. After a several moments, Mariah had control of her mind again. Instead of focusing on Derek and all his negative energy, she let her mind float back to the charming coach who had carried her books this morning. It was time for her to focus on the positive.

Time for something new and better.

Sadness over her broken relationship formed a ball in the pit of her stomach, but a rogue thought made her giggle through her tears.

Maybe something in gray sweatpants.

"Tannis! You should have warmed up more! Do you want to injure that arm?"

Coach Garcia felt like a song stuck on repeat. Didn't these guys ever listen when he told them to warm up?

"I did, Coach!" Tannis protested.

"No, you didn't. I can tell by the way you're throwing. Go back to the bullpen and warm up. Xiao! You are up!"

"Coach!" Tannis whined.

"No arguing! Git!"

Tannis slapped his glove against his leg and stormed off as the lean Ken Xiao took the pitcher's mound with a tight grin. The kid was always eager to take over and hone his skills, and he *had* spent his time in the bullpen warming up.

"Ok, let's start again!" Cole hollered.

Some days he wondered how he managed to keep his voice, yelling as much as he did. And it was the only time he yelled. His older sister once joked, asking him if his athletes responded to whispers.

And Cole had to agree. He had never been the yelling sort. To end up as a coach, hollering at baseballers all day . . .

Unfortunately for Xiao, he pitched for less than a half hour before Cole called practice.

He had lied a bit to his players. Cole didn't have a meeting; he just needed a break. The past couple of weeks had taken a lot out of him. His new dog had fallen off the couch and broke his leg, and while he was dealing with that, his girlfriend decided she wanted more attention and left.

The relationship broke but the pup's leg healed up well, and now Tavi the chocolate lab was back to running. He was a great running partner for Cole and had even brought Tavi to the track once or twice to run with his players who adored him. Not that he told admin about *that*. Tavi was a great dog, and Cole considered himself a nice guy. Why had he ended up with someone so self-centered?

Cole needed a night to vent, to drink, to lose himself. Tonight was that night.

By the time the stinking young men finished their showers and left the locker room, it was nearing five. Cole was beat. He missed lunch and if he didn't watch it, he wouldn't get out of the office until late.

"Screw it," he said to no one and slammed his notebook shut. The numbers would still be there in the morning.

Grabbing his duffel bag, he slammed the light switches down and left. A frosty beer was calling his name.

He cut over the grassy knoll to the parking lot and stopped short.

Professor Lenski was at the parking lot. *Mariah*, he reminded himself. Unconsciously he swiped his hand over his wavy black hair and approached her. Did she drop something again?

When he walked closer, he could see she wasn't picking something up, she was sitting on the edge of the curb. Crying.

Why was she crying?

"Mariah?"

She gasped and spun around, wide-eyed as if she'd done something wrong. The late afternoon sun was low in the western sky and created a halo around her. Cole was momentarily taken aback by the sheer beauty of the image she presented. The sad, broken, beautiful image, a figure from a painting.

"Are you Ok? Did you hurt yourself?"

Mariah wiped her face with the sleeve of her long sweater coat.

"Oh, Cole. No, nothing. I'm fine."

She wasn't fine. *Why do women say that?*

"I can see you're *not* fine," he said, settling onto the curb next to her. "You might feel better if you share it."

She flicked her dark eyes westward, squinting into the sunlight.

"You're probably busy and want to get home. I'm Ok."

"The only thing waiting for me at home is my dog. And as great as he is, I'm not in any hurry."

He rested his hands on his knee and kept his gaze light but engaged, studying her face as she considered his words.

"It's stupid," she finally said, dropping her face to study her boots. "I broke up with this toxic sort of guy. He got mad and broke one of my teacups. It was my favorite, and I'm crying over the broken cup."

Once again, Cole had to hold back a smile. He shifted his shoulders toward her.

"You're not crying over the guy? But over the teacup?"

Mariah huffed out a tittering laugh and wiped her cheeks again. Her entire hand was wrapped in her sleeve. She might have been speaking the truth, but Cole had the sense something else was going on.

"Yeah. I got it at an estate sale. The only one left of the set. It was just so pretty, dainty, like an English high-tea cup. The guy? I'll miss the companionship, but the guy not so much."

"Well, any guy who would break your favorite teacup seems like a dick."

This time she burst out laughing, that belly laugh from earlier. Cole tipped his head at her. Listening to that laugh was relaxing and likable. And he had an idea that he'd rather listen to that laugh than drink alone.

"Want to get a drink?" he asked suddenly. "Rant about your ex? Talk about teacups?"

Mariah stiffened, but the curl to her lips remained.

"What? Are you sure? That doesn't sound like fun for you."

"I'm a good listener, and I'm always down for a drink after a bad day. Let me put my gear away, go home and let my dog out, and we can meet at D'Canters wine bar at the mall?"

Her dark eyes studied him, and Cole straightened like he was under consideration for an award. Her eyes narrowed and he thought she'd say no. Fresh break up and all. Then she nodded.

"Yeah. I'll meet you there in a half hour?"

"Sounds like a plan," he told her as he stood and held out a hand to help her up.

And she took it.

Charming

Chapter Three

MARIAH RACED HOME, threw her bag on her bed, and plugged in her curling iron. She had less than thirty minutes to do something with her rat's nest of hair and touch up her make-up before meeting him.

Strange, but she craved his offer. She wasn't in a place to date again — not the same day she kicked out Derek. But she and Derek had only dated a few months, and this way she wouldn't sit at home alone and cry. Plus, she could continue to slyly admire Cole's tight form in his sweats. The mere thought of him sent a titillating shiver from her chest to her thighs. Drinks with Cole would be the perfect distraction.

Charming

The wine bar was a soothing locale with a décor dripping in deep red and dark wood, lined with wine bottles from around the world. A private place, an intimate place with dim lighting, a subdued weeknight crowd, and a relaxed atmosphere. Just what she needed after the day she'd had.

However, she didn't register much of the bar. Cole was already seated at a bar-height table.

He had arrived at the wine bar before her and had changed clothes as well. Fitted jeans replaced his sweats, and while she missed the sweats, it should have been illegal for him to wear denim that clung to his legs that way. His standard blue polo brought out the bronzed tone of his skin and made his eyes seem lighter. A dark shadow of a tattoo played peek-a-boo under his shirt sleeve.

Her eyes had a mind of their own as she sunk into the high-backed stool next to him. She hoped she managed to hide it, but she couldn't stop staring. The man was built like a god. It made sense, a coach and all, but his ass was carved from marble, Mariah was sure of it.

His thick chest begged to touched, and the dimple near his chin stood out in the shadows of the bar when he smiled. A dimple! His flawless smile and hazel eyes made it seem like no one else existed in the world when he turned to look at her.

That alone would make for a better night than being at home by herself.

He was the epitome of handsome, and a moment of self-consciousness wafted over Mariah. She often felt like a mess, and here she was, having a drink with a man who would give Superman a run for his money.

Mariah patted her green duster and decided to let all that go and enjoy the moment. She needed it after that shitty relationship she'd left.

"Mariah! Perfect timing. The wine list just arrived."

He stood up and kissed her cheek. A surprising flutter rose in her chest. *It's because he's new and I'm vulnerable,* she cautioned herself.

"I'll take a red blend," she told him, and he ordered a bottle for them to share.

"Not a beer?" she asked. "Don't athletes prefer beer? Or is that a stereotype?"

His sinfully sexy mouth angled up. "Nope, pretty accurate actually. But when in Rome –" He waved his hand around the Tuscan-styled bar.

"Understood. Thank you again for inviting me out. This is a sight better than pouting over an ex at home."

"I can't disagree. I had a breakup a few weeks ago."

"Is that why you got the dog?"

Cole licked his smiling lips. "No. The dog came before the breakup. He's just getting a lot more attention now."

So, no wife, no girlfriend. Maybe kicking Derek out had been a matter of serendipity – karma working in her favor. Even if it was merely this one date, Mariah was grateful for the company. It was such a change from the one-sided Derek-centered conversations with her ex.

Stop thinking about Derek!

Her heart warmed at having someone focused on her, gaze at her with those intense, whiskey-hued eyes . . . She shivered and hoped it didn't show on the outside.

Charming

When the bottle of red arrived, the waiter poured heavy and Cole lifted his glass. Mariah clinked her glass against his and drank deeply. In no time, they polished off their glasses of wine together, shared a plate of chicken wings and cheese sticks, complained about their students, and laughed the night away.

If only every breakup could end with a night of drinking with the sexiest man on campus.

"I'm surprised that I don't know you better, before now I mean," Cole told her as his dreamy face with his chiseled cheek bones made her chest flutter. *I need this,* she thought. *After all the shit with Derek, Cole is the distraction I need.*

"Why do you say that? It's not like we're in the same department or anything."

"No," he agreed, "but you seem to have my players in your classes every semester. Your Rate-My-Professor score must be sky high."

Her cheeks burned with a modest blush. "It is. I have a near perfect score."

Cole's deep laugh resonated across the table. "That makes sense. Athletes make recommendations to incoming freshmen, too. So, if one player liked you, then you probably will see a bunch of athletes in your classes."

"That would explain it. Either way, I'm glad they like my class." Mariah had finished her wine and now sipped the rest of her water. Then she grabbed her handbag and placed a light hand on Cole's sturdy arm.

"I should go. I don't have class until ten tomorrow, but I have a stack of papers that won't grade themselves."

34

"That's a perk to coaching. A lot of paperwork in general, but I don't have to grade tests or homework. I'll take that trade off. Are you Ok to drive? Do you want a ride home? Or an Uber?"

"I've only had one glass. We've been here three hours and I've been drinking water for the last hour. I'm in the clear. How about you?"

"Three hours?" Cole's forehead furrowed, and he nodded. "It probably seems like a teetotaler thing, but it's something I grind into my kids. Don't over imbibe. Don't drink and drive, and I practice what I preach. Can I at least walk you to your car?"

Who is this guy? He seemed impossible. Concerned, thoughtful, a role model to college students, looked like Adonis. Mariah had a flash that she wished she could meet a guy like Cole. He would be a huge improvement over jerks like Derek.

Then she realized that she hadn't met a guy *like* Cole. She met Cole. Maybe it was a sign.

He kissed her cheek goodbye before she left — nice, not overtly sexual, and cordial.

But the spot where his lips touched her cheek burned.

Mariah hoped she didn't blush too furiously. But in that moment, she made a decision.

And after she took a couple of days to recoup from her sudden break up, she might see if Cole was interested in more. He may have kissed her in a friendly way, but she was willing to take it to the next level.

After all, the best way to get over someone is to get under someone else.

35

Charming

And she really wanted to get under Cole.

She had strutted in like she owned the bar. That was one of the first things Cole noticed about Mariah — Professor Lenski to his players. Rare was a woman who exuded confidence as easily as she breathed, and here this stunning woman, who just went through a breakup, approached the table like it was any other Tuesday.

Fitted leggings. Boots to her knees.

Her hair was smoothed a bit and shimmered in the candlelight. Cole tried his best to stare into her eyes and study the light in her hair. Otherwise, she'd see how his gaze kept dropping to her breasts that popped from her tank top like ripe peaches on a tree. And when she leaned over the table, her cleavage practically begged to be admired.

And *oh*, he admired it.

Then when she looked at his face again, he'd flick his eyes back up like nothing had happened.

How had someone messed up with her? What was wrong with the guy she broke up with? From their conversation, it seemed she tried to sound fair and balanced. She slipped and called him toxic a couple of times, but then glossed over it, claiming she and her recent ex "just weren't right for each other."

His loss.

And Cole's gain.

The one drawback that Cole could see was the timing. *The worst timing ever.*

While his breakup happened weeks ago, it hadn't been a long-term thing and he'd had a few dates since. Nothing serious. Nothing that struck him like a baseball to the head, like Mariah had.

And she'd been right here on campus, the entire time!

Cole was more than willing to give her the time she needed before he asked for another date, but he made sure to get her digits before she drove off. He risked kiss on her cheek. Nothing demanding, nothing other than a friendly kiss. And he made a promise to himself not to call or text her back right away — he was going to let things develop on her timetable, not his.

He didn't need to complicate things for her.

But he wanted to. Cole wanted every complicated second he could have. Enough time to get in more than a kiss. Or at least a better one.

He stood in the parking lot after she drove away, the slight chill in the spring air refreshing after the heat of the day. And it helped cool the heat that had been building inside him the longer he was with her. Like she was a match that lit him on fire. He opened his mouth and inhaled that cool air to compose himself before he drove home.

It hadn't been a date. It had been a mutual night of ranting about ex's and students and school admin. And wine.

By God, it had felt like a date.

He walked in the fresh air to his pickup, his mind a whirl of numbers. How many days, weeks, did he need to wait before he did ask her out on a date? A real date? One with more than a kiss on the cheek?

A hell of a lot more than a kiss?

Campus just got very interesting.

Chapter Four

OVER THE NEXT several days, Mariah kept busy. The first thing she did was scour her apartment of anything that reminded her of Derek. Gifts, few though they were, pics from her phone, and any changes she'd made to accommodate him in her apartment – gone. Sheets – washed. Any clothing or bathroom items he'd left behind – in a box by the front door.

Mariah had let him linger too long as it was. She wasn't going to let him take up space in her apartment, or her mind, any longer.

And she had a lot to distract her from any emotional roller coaster of a breakup. Students were submitting their papers before their final essay was assigned, and on Thursday morning, as she stepped from her morning class, Tannis caught up with her. His light brown hair blew in the wind under his MLC baseball cap.

"Prof L? Can I ask you about my essay?"

Mariah hiked her knock-off designer bag higher onto her shoulder. The poor kid. He tried hard, but writing was not his strong suit. Plus, his time was limited. He was on her athletic roster and had to follow up with admin about his grades and attendance each month.

Thinking about Tannis and the baseball team brought the image of Cole to her mind. She shoved it away to focus on Tannis.

"Of course, Tannis. What's going on? Have you met with the tutor yet?"

Tannis held out his essay — two sheets of ragged paper with a smattering of incomprehensible sentences. Red marks scarred the paper, comments from the tutor. Mariah pointed to the comments.

"Yeah. I actually got Sabrina from class! She's a good tutor and made a lot of recommendations. You said we get extra credit if we go to the tutor. How do I do that?"

"Ok, did you get a slip from the tutor, a summary slip?"

Tannis's eyes lowered to his paper. "Um, I'm not sure."

Mariah pressed her fingers to her forehead, trying to make this process as easy as possible for the young man. Her greatest desire was for all her students to be successful in her class. Tannis included. He was on an athletic scholarship, after all. His grades mattered.

"I'm sure Sabrina signed one, but if you can't find it, how about this? Can you make sure to hand in that tutor copy of your essay when you hand in your final draft? Just staple it to the final. Then I can give you the extra credit."

His boyish face lit up. "Really?"

"And, because you went to the tutor, you might find your paper is better, and can earn you a higher grade. I'm glad you were able to find the time to make it to the tutor."

"Yeah, thanks for that. I don't want to lose my place on the team. Coach will kill me if I get put on academic probation. And my parents will kill me if I lose my scholarship. But college is hard, right?"

A heated flush coursed through Mariah at the mention of the Coach. He played for Cole. She knew Tannis played for his team but didn't let that connection affect her until now. She gave Tannis a distracted nod.

"It is, Tannis. But you're doing everything you should. Just keep trying. And keep asking for help when you need it. That's what your professors are here for."

"Ok," Tannis answered, not loving her response. "And the final draft of this paper is due Tuesday morning?"

"Right. Eight a.m. sharp."

"Ok. Thanks, Prof L."

Tannis gripped his wrinkled essay as he jogged off toward the baseball fields. Practice didn't start until the afternoon, so he was probably going to ask the coach a question. Or provide evidence of his commitment to his academics. Mariah's eyes followed his trail. From her vantage at the side of the humanities building, she could observe Tannis as he made for the baseball diamond.

If she wasn't mistaken, Cole stood at the center of the field, his rock-hard body showcased in another set of dark blue sweats and a matching MLC t-shirt.

She sighed at the sight. *Sighed*! What was wrong with her? She had never experienced such a visceral reaction to someone as she did to Cole. Like she was one of her co-eds that she was teaching.

Mariah had spent the previous night drinking wine and grading homework. Maybe it was time to see if Cole wanted to meet up again.

Watching Cole speak to Tannis, Mariah decided to text him that afternoon. *Time to get under someone,* she thought wickedly.

A text came through Cole's phone as he placed his lips to his whistle. Spring fever had hit his players hard. That was the only excuse Cole could find for why they were playing like this was little league and not college ball. And his frustrations grew with every missed catch, every dropped ball, every strike. He blew the whistle and all his players halted where they stood.

"You guys. We have a game tomorrow afternoon. Come on."

As a coach, he could be hard, tough when needed, but he always built to it — made sure he had a sound reason to let any angry or frustrated words fly. His mother had raised him to be a respectful man, and he extended that respect to his players.

Until they didn't deserve that respect anymore.

And they were pushing it.

"You need to focus! Where are your heads?"

"Coach, we are!" Ken piped up from the bullpen. His teammates grumbled in agreement.

"No, you aren't. Look at you — it's like everyone's attention is somewhere else, and whatever you are doing, you're not focusing on the very thing you should be. The *ball*."

At least his players had the good sense to drop their faces and find their cleats suddenly interesting.

"We are going to go one more round, another set of plays, and we'll see where we're at. Grosseman College might seem like a lesser team, but we barely scraped by last time we played them."

The team grumbled again, this time agreeing with Cole.

Thank God, he thought. Maybe the reminder of their last near miss would light a fire under their asses.

And he was rewarded. The MLC Hawks picked up their feet and played like the winners he knew they were. Satisfied they would have a better end to their practice, Cole pulled his phone from his pocket. The text notification read Mariah.

Cole licked the inside of his lips. He *had* made an impression on the curly-haired writing professor. And evidently, she was ready to move on after her recent break-up.

Always better to get right back on that horse, Cole well knew. But from experience, he also knew that sometimes, a break-up needed more time. He didn't want to come across as pushy, but he had already decided that if she didn't text, he was going to this weekend. Fortunately for him, she beat him to the punch after two days.

— I had a great time Tuesday. Thanks again for the wine and the ear.

Low-key enough. Cole texted back.

— Me too. Are you doing Ok?

Three blinking dots. Cole did a quick scan of his team. Tannis's throw to home was solid. Cole nodded approvingly and returned his focus to his phone.

— I don't know if you are interested, but would you want to try and meet up again this weekend?

Ahh, there it was. His patience had paid off. Cole ran his hand through his midnight-black hair and smiled to no one in particular.

— That sounds like a plan. I have a bb game Friday afternoon and usually take the players out for pizza after. I can do a late Friday. I got Sat open too.

Wow, that was probably more information than she needed.

— How about Saturday afternoon? We can do an early dinner or something?

An early dinner sounded perfect. He texted that back and offered to pick her up. Was this a real date? Or did she want to meet up instead? Was he taking her text the wrong way? Misinterpreting it? Fucking lack of context.

Then her address flashed onto his screen.

Charming

His mouth edged up in a half-smile and he rubbed at the light black stubble on his jaw.

It *was* a date.

Charming

Chapter Five

MARIAH FORCED HERSELF to calm down, telling herself that it was just a date, but Cole had done everything right at their wine bar meetup, so her expectations were skyrocketing.

How had he done that? Or did it just *seem* right after her trauma with Derek?

In truth, she really didn't care.

Cole had arrived on time, devilishly dashing in his red and black button down and black pants. He had waited while she grabbed her long sweater, this one black with draping sleeves, to throw over her clinging charcoal-gray pencil dress. With her heeled boots, she was barely an inch shorter than he was.

When they reached the car, she made to open her door, but Cole rushed in and opened it for her. Mariah's mind whirled. *When was the last time a guy opened a door for me?* It smacked of gender stereotyping, but for a date, she didn't care. On a date, it smacked of manners.

They ordered a light dinner of salads and soup, nachos for appetizers, and margaritas. He told her about the game on Friday afternoon, griping about his players, but she noticed a touch of pride that shone in his face as he talked about them.

"So, you won anyway?"

The smile on Cole's face was infectious.

"Yeah. I mean, I thought we would. But I couldn't let them know that, you know? Once a player gets lazy, doesn't want to work, it's all downhill. If you want something, even if you think it's a guarantee, you still have to work for it as if it's the most difficult task. That's what I try to teach my players."

"That's a great behavior to model. For them, I mean." Mariah was fascinated by Cole's speech. Certain traits seemed completely absent from so many people today, at least in Mariah's limited view.

"That and respect," Cole continued. "I also try to respect them, you know? I hold respect in high esteem, and if I want them to respect me, I need to be able to respect them. So, with that comes honesty, hard work, everything."

"Wow, most people that I run into think coaches don't do anything other than run laps and play sports. Maybe yell at players or refs. Teaching anything above that? Not even on their register."

Cole raised a sleek black eyebrow. "By most people, you mean other faculty?"

Mariah shrugged and tipped her head, her silvery waves swinging. "The bane of administration. You know how it is. The staff versus the faculty versus athletics. And some departments see athletics as a waste of money and resources."

"How about you? Do you think the same? That coaches are all sweaty guys who run laps?"

Mariah eyed Cole over her margarita glass.

"Well, considering over a third of our coaches at MLC are women, I'm gonna say no. Do you think all writing professors are nerds with glasses who don't know how to socialize?"

Cole's face pinched for a moment, then relaxed. "Ouch. Yeah, I get what you mean. Is that what most people believe about you?"

She nodded as an aching memory of her ex tried to rise in her mind. He'd made a comment in those exact words once. Mariah shoved it to the side to focus on the handsome demi-god of a man sitting at the table with her. One whose words didn't cut her to the core.

His chiseled face, enticing smile, and sculpted chest were more than enough of a diversion. And the way his eyes danced as he gazed at her, exploring her with a singular focus .

. . Once again, they had engaging banter, deep conversation, and this time Cole opened up about the relationship he'd exited.

"All because of a dog?" Mariah asked. It seemed petty to leave because of an injured puppy.

Cole shrugged and gave her another smile that could melt an iceberg.

"She was on her way out. The dog was just an excuse."

"Tell me about Tavi," she asked.

A thrill electrified her at the expression on his face when she asked. *Who doesn't like a man who loves his dog?* she asked silently.

They lingered over dinner, and the longer they lingered, the closer their chairs became, until her shoulder pressed against his and Cole's hand rested on her bare thigh just below the hem of her dress. His finger brushed against hers in a fiery gesture, and it burned so hot, his skin on her skin. She wanted that fire to consume her.

Mariah barely recalled the conversation at dinner. When was the last time she experienced such an electric heat with a man? *Not with Derek. Not in a long while.*

Yes, she decided. *It's time to get under Cole.*

Then Cole glanced at her with his sparkling hazel eyes that caught the dim lighting, and a zap of electricity jolted through her, making her heart throb in her chest. Their gaze spun out, heat rising between them. Then his face was closer, those intense eyes never wavering, and he captured her lips in a long, sultry kiss. His hand slipped into her hair at the back of her neck, sending wave after wave of shivers down her spine.

If he could make her react like this with his hand on her neck, what else might he be able to do to her?

His tongue teased between her lips, bathing her tongue with the sweetness of salt and his margarita, and she sucked on it in response, getting drunk on his kiss. Cole inhaled her breath, and their lips parted, barely.

"Should I pay the bill?" he asked, still polite as hell.

She loved the deference. So much power contained in his pristine physique, and he tempered it perfectly. Nothing was sexier than a man holding back his power. His breath was a hot caress on her lips.

"Yes."

"Yes."

Her hands pressed over his thigh to his groin, brushing against his dick that pulsed so hard all the blood in his head was lost. His cock needed it all, and she must have felt his throbbing because her long-fingered hand squeezed lightly in response. He groaned and closed his eyes.

Then he lifted his head and his arm to the passing waitress. "Check please."

Cole didn't have time to think about where they were going next. They spilled into the parking lot, stumbling because their lips and hands were too busy. Mariah clutched his shirt in her curled fists, practically dragging him to the car.

"My place," she breathed into his mouth.

He had to take one hand off her ass that he could feel way too well through her thin dress. A dangerous type of dress that displayed every curve in a tempting buffet, he thought wildly as he pressed the fob and his truck lights flashed in the dark.

One more pulling kiss and he all but threw her into the cab, then ran, faster than he did in laps on the field, around the truck bed to the driver's seat. Thank God she only lived a few streets away. He wasn't sure he would have made it otherwise.

Mariah had her keys to her apartment ready when he parked, and she dropped everything — her purse, her keys, her long sweater that brushed her knees — into a pile by the door.

Cole closed the door with an earth shattering click. Mariah stood against him in the entryway. His body quivered, waiting until he couldn't wait anymore. He needed to be with her, in her — it seemed the world might end if he didn't.

He was done waiting. His finger toyed lightly at the upper curve of her breastbone.

"Yes?" he asked.

She grabbed his shirt in her fists again, crushing his strapping body to hers. Her lips were so close, but not touching. Not yet. Instead, she taunted him with that space between, pulling the space so taut it might break.

"Yes," she answered in a whisper.

Then his lips crushed hers, his tongue dancing in and out with her own, his teeth biting at her lips. With shocking force, he rammed her against the wall, locking her arms between them. One hand gripped her face under the line of her jaw; his other hand cupped her tight ass, clenching and unclenching.

Mariah's lips slid from his, down the open neck of his shirt to nip at the lightly haired skin of his chest.

His reaction rocked him to his core — he threw his head back and gasped at her boldly aggressive touch. Who knew that writing professors were assertive?

Cole forced her chin up, so she looked at him, her dark eyes liquid as she drank him in.

"Are you just going to tease me?" he panted.

Mariah shifted her hand from his shirt down his belly to the pulsating bulge under his zipper. She giggled low in her throat, a raspy version of that full laugh she had.

"Just until you beg."

She spoke into his chest, tickling his black chest hairs with her tongue before her hand constricted on his bulging rod. Cole groaned and slid his hand from her jaw to her left tit.

She knows just how to turn me on, just how to touch me, and I am helpless in her hands.

Cole's brain spun out of control, and if he weren't careful, he'd end up throwing her down and fucking her brains out right on the cheap tile floor of her front hall.

She had him begging all right. And they were still fully clothed. What would she do to him once she had him naked? If they even managed to get that far? All he wanted right now was for her to whip is dick out and ride it.

"Please," he finally whispered.

Charming

Chapter Six

KEEPING A FIRM grip on his shirt, she led him through the archway to her bedroom.

Mariah had spent the week eliminating any memory of her ex from her apartment, most specifically her bedroom. Clean sheets, a fresh comforter, emptied drawers. The one thing she did keep was the box of condoms that she had purchased the week before, still unopened. She was going to tear into that box tonight. It was time to bring fresh memories into her home.

Charming

Cole's impossibly broad shoulders barely fit through the narrow doorway. Once in the bedroom, she slowed herself just a bit.

His physique was toned, primed, at its peak. She'd been forced to admire it under jeans and sweats and t-shirts, and now she was going to enjoy the full view.

Had she ever had a man this hot, this perfectly chiseled in her bedroom before?

No. Honestly, she hadn't.

And she was going to enjoy this.

With painful deliberation, Mariah unfastened each black button of his shirt, exposing more and more of his pumped, bronzed chest.

At the last button, Cole whipped off his shirt and stood like a statue before her. Mariah made a show of stepping back to admire him.

Holy shit. He was a work of art, and her insides quivered at the prospect of seeing the rest of him.

She finally had a great view of his arm tat — a baseball inside a glove, artistically rendered. Simple and discreet when he wanted it to be. Mariah traced it with a curved fingernail.

Cole lifted an eyebrow in question and grabbed at his belt.

"Oh, yes," she told him.

With deft, capable fingers (*what else were those fingers capable of?*), he released his belt, unfastened his pants, and let them fall to the floor. Then in a flash, he looped his thumbs into his clinging boxer briefs that left little to the imagination, and they were off as well, until her bronze god stood before her.

Charming

Mariah licked her lips as her blood pounded in her head, her chest, her pussy, and thighs. Her knees shook — *shook!* — at the mere sight of him.

He could be a model. That was her first thought. And on the heels of that.

And I get to ride that tonight.

Every muscle was carved from marble, like an Italian statue. His powerful arms and chest narrowed to his tight abs, to those hip bones that her college roommate Anna once called "panty-droppers," and she hadn't been wrong. He was strong and formidable but kept it in check — and that measure of control was sexier than almost everything else about him.

Almost.

And if she weren't wet enough, his cock throbbed hugely before him.

Oh, hell yes, the man was blessed. Thick and long? Who the hell was gifted with both, and the body of a god to boot?

And he was in her room, getting ready to fuck her.

Sometimes, the world was just.

"Your turn," his deep voice resonated to her bones.

First her boots and clinging dress, followed by her matching lace bra and panty set.

She started for the bed, but he grabbed her hand to stop her.

"Not so fast. I want to get my view."

Mariah's lips curled to one side as she spun slowly, letting him take in her full breasts with dusky cinnamon nipples, the gentle swell of her belly that led to her fox-brown curls between her thighs.

Charming

Before she could finish her turn, he yanked her hand, pulling her against his burning skin, and claimed her mouth. His cock pulsed against her thigh. Releasing her hand, he grabbed her curvy backside with one hand while the other slid between their bodies, one broad finger finding the slit under her trimmed, bikini-style triangle of pubes.

His fingertip made long strokes in and out of her lower lips, dragging across her clit, then around her clit, then over again. He was a god in his body and with his hands. *Blessed indeed.*

Mariah's hand found his shoulders, and gripping so her fingernails left marks on his upper arms, she let the rest of herself fall back, trusting him so his one arm, one powerful, muscled god-like arm, held her upright.

Her body went lax, focusing on the sensation of weightlessness in his grip on her back and the feel of his finger between her legs. Then she began to vibrate and shudder — her heart beating between her legs — first low in her clit, then up through her belly until waves of fluttering vibrations reached her fingertips and toes, and she had to grit her teeth as she shrieked and moaned.

She expected him to race her to the bed, throw her down and find his climax.

Once again, Cole surprised her. With one tremendous hand, he held her close and waited for her to recover. When she opened her eyes in the dim light, Cole was gazing into her face, a mix of hard passion and soft enjoyment. He was sucking on his finger, and a sultry smile tugged at his cheeks.

With one weak hand, she took his finger from his mouth and licked the tip before swallowing it, tasting her own salty sweet juices.

The softness fled Cole's face, replaced with hard and hungry need.

Mariah popped his finger out of her mouth.

"Your turn," she whispered.

Mariah bent and made to go down on him, but Cole couldn't wait. He was ready to explode. Instead, he lifted her up by her underarms, and she knew in an instant what he wanted. She reached for her bedside table, and with her nimble fingers, rolled a condom on his long, pulsing cock.

She was tall, so it was easy for her to lift her legs to his hips as he settled her on the length of his dick. He slid in with rapturous ease.

Mariah was wet and ready for him, and as she clung to him where he stood in the center of her bedroom, the sensations they had were of skin on skin, of their heat, of building to their peaks. He gazed into her eyes as he moved inside her, their eyes joined just as their bodies joined. Nothing else existed, nothing touched but their rhythmic palpations and the slapping of their hips as he thrust and thrust and rubbed and rubbed, and she clung to him for dear life.

Finally, Cole couldn't hold himself back. He had started to lose control when she kissed him in the hallway, and with each motion he came closer and closer. Now he was done. Cole pressed and thrust harder, clenching her tighter and roaring deep in his chest — a primal sound that rocked him to his core. Only then did he slam his eyes shut. His dick erupted in spools of cum that poured and poured until his legs quivered.

Cole dropped his forehead to Mariah's as she panted along with him. She also dropped one leg for added support, and as he slipped out of her sheath, she dropped the other. Then she guided him blindly to her bed where he collapsed. Mariah fell onto the bed next to him, and they laid there for several moments, holding hands and catching their breaths.

Amazing. Amazing. Amazing. Oh God. For several heartbeats, that was all he could think.

He was a hot, sweaty mess, but he didn't care. Once he could focus again, he rolled to his side to face her.

Mariah's boobs shook with each deep breath she took, and he relished the view for a several seconds before tracing her nipples and the curve of her breasts with his finger. She shivered under his touch.

"It's like every nerve is on fire, and you are a live wire touching me," she whispered to him as goose bumps sprung up and her nipples tightened even more. Cole leaned over to kiss one nipple, then the other. Then he fell back onto the bed.

Now came the uncomfortable part. He'd come into the date with no expectations, not the least of which was to end up naked on Mariah's bed.

What came next? Was he a one-night stand? Were they going to try another date? Was she even ready for a relationship?

Charming

Though it still might be too soon, he kept his gaze on the ceiling and hoped it was the latter.

Not only was she a fun date, but she was also an amazing fuck, and he just wanted to *be* with her. Everything inside him wanted to be *with* her.

Suddenly she rolled on top of him, and cupping his face between her palms, she kissed him full on the lips — a light, sweet kiss so contrary to the heady passion they'd shared minutes ago. Cole wrapped his arms around her back and responded with the same gentle kissing.

Mariah stopped kissing him as quickly as she started, and with a sultry gleam, her fingertips moved over his skin, tracing his sinewy muscles — over his arms, across his chest, and down his waist to his abs.

"I've never been fucked by a god before," she told him matter of factly.

Cole burst into a laugh. He'd been complimented for his body, but this was the first time he'd been compared to a god.

"Well, then, mere mortal. Did it live up to your expectations?"

She squinted her eyes at him. Then she dipped her head to avert her gaze.

Charming

"I was afraid it was too soon. But when I saw you on Tuesday, you looked so fine in those sweats. Can I admit something embarrassing? Don't take it the wrong way?"

His lighthearted expression grew serious, and he brushed a bright lock of hair from her face. The gesture was so intimate, so gentle, her heart twinged. Sex was easy. That was just skin. Emotions were hard.

"You can tell me anything," he said in a tender voice, and Mariah almost lost it.

This man — he exuded every sense of power, command, force. He could take anything he wanted without effort, yet his demeanor, his caring gestures were the opposite. *Now I might cry,* Mariah thought.

"I should have felt something this week, but like you said about your ex, it was a long time coming. I didn't feel anything for him . . ." She paused, hesitating.

"But?" he compelled her to finish. She still couldn't look at him. Her waves of hair covered much of her face.

"Maybe this is too much, and if I'm reading too far into this, let me know. But everything I thought I should have felt about him, I feel about you instead. This, tonight?"

She lifted her eyes that shimmered in the darkness — from tears? From their lovemaking? From the weight of her own honesty?

Cole craved honesty. It was the foundation of respect. And if she were about to open up to him, maybe this wasn't some rebound. Maybe they had a chance together — a chance he was willing to take. He would do everything in his power to encourage her to be honest with him.

"Yeah?" His hands moved to her hair again, threading though it. Another movement that seemed even more intimate than the sharing of their bodies.

"I felt more tonight with you than I ever did with him."

Without a doubt, she could hear the pounding of his chest. Maybe this meant she was willing to take a chance on him as well.

"Can I be honest with you?" he asked. She nodded, biting at her lower lip. "I wasn't sure what you wanted tonight. A date? A one-night stand? The start of something? And I didn't want to pressure you. I was willing to take whatever you could offer."

Mariah tilted her head to the side, surveying him. Her phone buzzed and flashed a notification, but she ignored it. Cole's eyebrows lifted to his smooth black hair line.

"You're willing to work for it?" she asked, echoing his advice he'd mentioned earlier. "What if I want another date? What if I'm just a complicated mess? Can you work that hard? You don't think it's too soon?"

Cole lifted her hand and kissed her fingertips.

"You're a brilliant college professor. I would never presume to question your good judgment. And I would work for you every day, like it was the Olympics."

Her smile was so wide in the obscurity of the room that her white teeth beamed like a lighthouse on the sea.

Cole stayed the night. And most of the next day.

Charming

Chapter Seven

THEY HAD STUPIDLY agreed not to rush anything, but that didn't last at all. Cole spent most of the next week at Mariah's, or she at his place. They met up on campus as often as they could during the week, which meant walking her to her car after late classes on Mondays and Wednesdays, then lunch on Tuesdays and Thursdays as well. But to make sure nothing seemed inappropriate, they sat on opposite sides of the picnic table while they ate and appeared completely platonic. Or at least *thought* they appeared platonic.

Charming

Since they both worked for the college, Cole's coaching and game schedule left plenty of time for Mariah to grade, so when they were together, they could leave MLC on the campus. It was far too easy to gossip about students and admin when they weren't at school, and they tried not to.

Which was easy enough to do when they spent much of their time together in bed.

Cole was an insatiable animal, and Mariah encouraged it. *More leggings*, he had requested.

One evening, as Mariah was lying across his chest in her candlelit bedroom, Cole twined a thread of her hair around his finger. He seemed to like her unruly curls. His hands were always in them, touching them, brushing at them.

"Do you want to come to a game?" he asked, breaking the thick, post-sex quiet.

Mariah lifted her head over him, and her hair spilled around their faces in a pale curtain. Cole blew several strands of hair from his mouth.

"Really? You aren't worried your players might see something between us?"

Cole shrugged one rugged shoulder. "What if they do?"

And really, students had to have noticed them on campus. This was just the next step.

"We work for different departments, so there's technically nothing in the HR manual against this." Mariah licked her lips and flicked her finger back and forth between them. "It might be frowned upon, though."

"Are you kidding? The Athletic Director is married to the Dean of the Arts department! I think the admin will overlook this. As long as we aren't caught making out in the cafeteria, we should be Ok."

Mariah tapped her finger on his chest, letting his logic sink in. He wasn't wrong — but they both had something to lose if the administration decided they didn't like their relationship. His golden eyes flicked over her.

"Have you ever been to one of our ball games before?" he asked, focusing the conversation back to his initial question.

Mariah shook her head. "Nope. But then, I was never invited before either."

Cole's thick lips curled up at her suggestion. "I'm inviting you, then. I would love to have you see a game. And I know of at least two players who have you as their writing teacher."

It was Mariah's turn to smile. She traced Cole's pouty lips with a gentle fingertip. "Tannis and Enrique. And I would love to watch a game."

Cole lifted his torso from the bed a few inches, so his face came closer to hers.

"This Friday? If you aren't too busy?"

"Some essays that can wait until Saturday morning," she answered and drove her lips against his.

The sun bore down relentlessly on the players and fans on a humid, early May afternoon. Mariah tied her sweater around her waist and fanned herself with a random folder she had in her bag. Her seat was in the full sun — no shade was to be had on the bleachers. The baseball game was nearly over, and this time the Mount Laguna Hawks dominated, entering the 9th with a score of 8-1.

Before the game, Mariah had asked if she should come up to him after the game, or if it would be better if she left and congratulated him later.

"Thank you for the vote of confidence," he said in his booming voice, "but we haven't exactly been discreet on campus. My players probably already know something is going on. I mean, I'm not going to hide you."

She had smiled widely and slipped a gratified kiss on his soft, full lips.

His words held a ring of truth. Another professor in the English department who had a non-regular position as a librarian as well, had winked boldly at Mariah one afternoon when Cole had walked her to her next class. An email not ten minutes later hit her inbox. Charlotte wanted all the details. Mariah promised to give additional information later.

People on campus had an idea that the baseball coach was "hitting that" — if she used her students' punny vernacular. But she didn't. Mariah blushed around Cole enough without that rumor ringing in her head.

Mariah let her mind peruse that while at the game. Her mind spun at the fact that more people, students, or faculty, hadn't commented. Perhaps they were just being discrete. Even though it wasn't frowned upon for faculty and staff to date, there was still a taboo element, especially to be sleeping with someone as well-known and beloved on campus as Coach Garcia. Could she get fired? Cole didn't seem to think so, as long as they managed the relationship without it impacting their presence on campus.

During the lulls between innings, she graded stacks of homework and tried to remain focused on the chicken-scratch of sentences balanced on her lap. It made forgetting everything else in her life easier. Especially calls from Derek.

The texts and phone calls from her ex had become almost combative. Mariah had never dealt with someone who didn't leave when a relationship ended, and she didn't know what to do about Derek's non-stop barrage of notifications.

Mariah wanted to tell Cole about it. But why? To give him a heads up? Solicit his advice? To what end? She and Cole were just starting to date. Plus, this was her problem, and the sooner she handled Derek, the better. But that would mean answering one of those texts or calls, and Mariah wasn't ready for that. She had decided to give it a few more days to settle. If Derek didn't by then, she'd tell him off completely and hope he got the hint. If nothing else, she could block him to stop his contact. She didn't want to change her number, but if it got to that point, she'd do it in a heartbeat.

Otherwise, it might become the type of problem where she would need to tell Cole. And Mariah didn't want that to happen — she didn't want to be the drama-queen girlfriend. Her jaw tightened, shooting pain into her neck just thinking about it. They had enough to consider just dating on campus.

The word *girlfriend* caught in her mind, and she flicked her eyes to the Adonis-like coach studying the plays from the sidelines. His entire body was clenched in focus and readiness, and the muscles of his arms bulged under his jersey that hugged his chest. *Girlfriend*. They were dating, that much

69

Mariah knew. And she was exclusive with Cole. Could she go as far as to call him her boyfriend? Juvenile as it may have sounded to her ears, Mariah's heart fluttered and she flushed each time she thought of referring to Cole as her boyfriend.

He'd been everything Mariah was looking for in a partner, and she wasn't about to mess that up by letting her ex's annoying behavior get in the way. Cole deserved more than a melodramatic relationship with the local college professor.

Staring at him distracted her from her chaotic thoughts and from her grading. Once she realized she was making dopey eyes at him, like a charmed schoolmarm, Mariah shook her head and scanned the stands, hoping no one caught her.

The final crack of the bat meant that the Hawks scored two additional runs in the bottom of the 9th, and cheers erupted, complete with metallic banging of feet on the bleachers. The Hawks had won again and sealed their position in the playoffs in two weeks.

Mariah made her way down to the bullpen that opened out the back and led to the locker rooms. Cole was still near that door, talking to some other players. Most had left, but three players, including Tannis, let their gloves dangle by their sides as they listened to Coach.

Charming

Tannis did a comical double-take upon seeing Mariah. She nodded at him but remained off to the side, waiting for Cole.

Once he was done with coaching duties, Cole turned to Mariah with a wide smile. Tannis, however, beat him to the punch and stepped toward her.

"Professor L! Hey! Did you watch the game?"

He was all teeth and dimples at the prospect of having one of his professors in attendance, and Mariah's lips pulled into a soft smile of her own.

"Yes, Tannis. I was invited to watch, so I had to come and see this great baseball team of ours."

Tannis's face screwed up in confusion.

"You were invited? So, you aren't here to talk to me about something for class?"

Mariah gave a slight laugh and flicked her gaze to Cole's dancing eyes. Tannis whipped his head back and forth from Cole to Mariah and back, then burst out in a fake sounding guffaw and slapped his thigh with his glove.

"Coach! You dog! Look at you, going after Professor L!"

"Reyes! Watch your mouth!" Cole tried to sound critical, but the blush that covered his cheeks hid nothing. Tannis kept laughing.

"Alright! I'll head to the locker rooms. Should I tell the other players to wait for your post-game victory speech? Or are you going to be too busy—"

Tannis waggled his eyebrows, and Cole slapped his back with a wide hand. Tannis ran for the lockers.

"I'll be there in a minute!" he shouted after Tannis.

Charming

The kid stopped and gaped at his coach.

"Come on, Coach! It'll take more than a minute, I'd hope!" he yelled before spinning in that athletically graceful way he had and racing for the locker room before the coach could lambast him.

Cole didn't even try. He'd dropped his face into his hands, his cheeks red against his tanned skin. Mariah reached around his trim waist and hugged him.

"Congrats on the win," she said into his neck, and he grinned, pleased at the outcome.

"Did you enjoy it? The game?"

She laughed at his tone — he reminded her of an excited little boy.

"There were some low points, but overall, I did enjoy it! You're a great coach. Your players did well."

Cole glanced at the exit. "Except when they're cracking jokes about us."

"They were bound to find out eventually," she commented.

Cole shifted his hands to wrap his arms around Mariah, her curves melting into the sharp definition of his chest.

"Yeah, but I had hoped you weren't going to be around when they made their inappropriate jokes."

Mariah shrugged. "I've heard worse."

She lifted her face to his dusty, sweat-stained one. He was not the type of coach who sat in the bullpen during the game. He was on his feet, running back and forth, commenting on game strategy with every run, every catch, and he looked as though he'd played the entire game himself. She tasted grit on his lips when he kissed her.

"You are Ok with your players seeing us together? You realize this means the whole campus will know by Monday."

"Like you said," Cole answered with a smile, "they were bound to find out. And I'm glad it's out in the open. I didn't like feeling like I was sneaking around."

"Neither did I. If any students or admin ask, are you Ok with me referring to you as my boyfriend?"

Cole pressed her away from his chest and gazed at her with a cockeyed look.

"Hell, I hope so. I've been calling you my girlfriend for over a week now."

This time, Mariah's belly laugh rang out, and she threw her arms around his neck to kiss more of the grit from his mouth.

"Ok," she said, reluctantly pulling her lips from his. "Time to go lecture your players. They will have enough to gossip about with you being here with me for as long as you have."

Cole stepped away, moving toward the exit and the locker rooms. When he smiled, a teasing dimple played peek-a-boo in his cheek. "No, they'll gossip as to why I didn't keep you longer."

Then he ran off, the tinkling sound of Mariah's laughter following him to the lockers.

Charming

Her text inviting Cole over to her place was expected but still sent a thrill through his chest. Nothing better than capping off a win than by celebrating with someone.

Not just anyone, his someone. *Mariah.*

And he believed there was a great chance they'd be celebrating in her bed.

No wonder there was an allure to campus romances for college students — just thinking about Mariah teaching a few buildings over, seeing her as she rushed from class to class on campus — the surreptitious nature of their relationship made it even hotter. Now to be campus gossip? Cole thought that was exciting as hell.

And to top that off, Mariah surprised him more each day.

Stereotypes were difficult to dispel. And most stereotypes about coaches were the "dumb jock" type of comments. Mariah had her own stereotypes to work with, and Cole had to admit he was guilty of some of them.

Instead of a geeky girl who preferred classical music and spent her free time in a library, Mariah listened to classic rock and spent her free time playing all sorts of games, from video to board to computer games. And she could curse harder than most of his players! Of course, reading was her preferred way to pass the time, and she'd given him a bawdy response when he commented on the size of her bookcase.

She was nothing like he expected, but everything he wanted. He hadn't planned on falling for the writing professor, yet here he was, wondering what surprise she had for him now. Her text was enigmatic at best. Just like Mariah.

"Come in," she called from the other side of the door when he knocked.

From the dappled light and heady scent of linen and vanilla candles, Cole knew a good night was definitely on the horizon. He was smart enough to know what lit candles on a date night meant.

But the vision of Mariah leaning against the kitchen entry in nothing but a red and white apron froze him at the doorway. A throbbing rush rose from his groin to his head. Cole had just enough presence of mind to kick the door shut behind him as he entered.

"Mariah." His voice was a choked whisper.

Enigma was too light a word. Then she smiled, a sultry, half-curved smile, and he was lost. She held his cock and his heart in her bare hands, and she didn't even know it. He'd have to let her know, sooner rather than later.

"Hey babe." Mariah's voice was liquid, the finest whiskey poured from a well-aged bottle, hot and smooth and refined all at once. "Your team did a great job today, due to your amazing coaching, and you deserve a reward."

Cole stepped to her and traced his finger over the trim on the apron. "What's my reward?" he asked, his voice husky.

"I made steaks for dinner. They are keeping warm in the oven. I hope you didn't eat too much pizza with your players."

A hard breath puffed from Cole's chest.

"You can't begin to think I can eat with you looking like this?"

"Yeah. I figured as much."

Then she went to the arm of her love seat couch and bent over. *Bent over!* Her plump ass was the most mind-numbing invitation and Cole could do nothing but groan.

"Come ride me from behind," she commanded. "Don't make me ask twice."

Cole lost it. He rushed her, unbuttoning his pants with one hand as he grasped her butt cheek in the other. He'd been hard since he'd walked in the door, his dick painfully straining against his jeans, and releasing his aching bulge drove him to the brink of madness.

And that madness crashed in his head, rattled his body, and pulsed in his cock, and he dove into her welcome softness that sucked warm, wet, and tight. He groaned through his entire body as he sunk in deep.

His hands at first traced the contours of her body, down her back and over the pale globes that led to her thighs. He gripped the plush skin where her hips rounded into her ass, his hands sinking into her curves with eager hunger — desperate, covetous, compelling hunger that could only be satiated by Mariah's body. Cole held onto her as though there was nothing remaining in the world, as if the foundations of the earth fell away and if he let go, he would fall into nothingness.

She asked for nothing in return, taking him all in, gasping and moaning as he rode her until he blew his wad deep inside her. He clenched and collapsed across her back, wondering if he would ever breathe or think normally again.

Chapter Eight

MARIAH MARVELED AT Cole. He hadn't lied. He'd said he would work like he was in training for the Olympics, and *OH MY GOD*, did he.

From the little things, like opening her door, to the big things like how adventurous and attentive he was in bed (*and between her legs!*). The sex was astounding — forceful, commanding, and undeniably fulfilling. At times it seemed to Mariah that she could never get enough of Cole.

Charming

Just being in his presence was a note-worthy moment. He exuded a sense of ease and calm, like slipping into a warm bath away from all the miserable in the world. Away from grading. Away from demands from admin. Away from reminders of her ex.

Cole was doing everything Derek should have been doing — so much so that she rarely thought about her ex. A jolting shock of embarrassed heat pounded in her head whenever she ruminated on how long she had stayed with that narcissist. In fact, she had gleaned much of those realizations about her ex when she discussed him with Cole. Whether from that ripe sense of embarrassment or something deeper, she didn't know. She wasn't a psych professor. All she knew was she wanted to put Derek into a little box and dump it in the garbage, so she didn't have to think about him again.

The one thing stopping her from doing that was her phone blowing up. With calls and texts from Derek. Mariah had blocked him on all her social media, just to avoid a situation like this. But then he started calling and texting from other numbers . . .

Mariah also noticed that Cole's gaze flicked to her phone at those notifications, and her chest dropped to her stomach every time it happened. He tried to hide it from her, and when it was just one or two notifications, he ignored it like anyone else might.

But on the nights where the texts were non-stop, his amber gaze drifted over to her phone more often.

One night when they were cuddling on the couch, enjoying a subdued date of eating popcorn and watching a movie, her phone didn't stop. Mariah had to silence it before slamming it face-down on the arm of the couch, and she made sure to keep her pursed lips of frustration turned away from Cole. He averted his eyes away quickly, but not quickly enough. She didn't miss the moue of distress on his face.

"My ex," she explained vaguely, turning her attention back to the T.V. screen. "He keeps texting me to see if he left things here. I've just been ignoring him."

"Is it getting bad? Do we need to do something?"

Her heart melted at the "we" comment, but she didn't want to deal with any Derek drama tonight.

"No, I'll just keep ignoring them and he'll stop."

That should be a good explanation, she thought. Mariah didn't want to upset Cole by telling him that her ex was asking to meet up. Or that the texting was getting out of hand. She would handle it.

But she also knew that her explanation wasn't good *enough*. Cole deserved to know what was going on. Hiding it from him was not going to make their relationship stronger. If anything, she cringed on the inside, feeling like she was lying.

Cole appeared to accept the answer and his whole body relaxed. He caught her eye with his and grasped her hand, threading his fingers through hers. Tethering her to him. Claiming her.

I'll tell him soon, she promised herself. *But not tonight.*

Mariah nestled into his solid mass and lost herself in the movie.

Her phone didn't stop. At first, Cole hadn't registered it — everyone's phone dings or vibrates throughout the day. Cole's players hated that he made them keep their phones in their lockers during practice. Once he'd explained they needed to focus on the game at hand and not some electric green bubble on their screens, his players had grudgingly accepted the decree. They didn't like it, but they respected him enough to accept it.

The continual dinging was what bugged Cole. The phone didn't stop. While Mariah had told him that her ex was asking if he left anything behind, that should have died out, at least in his experience.

Instead, the notifications grew worse.

He didn't let it bother him. He *tried* not to let it bother him.

But why so many texts?

Was something else going on?

What was she not telling him?

The worst wasn't that she might be hiding the full truth. No, people hedged all the time for any number of reasons. Yet, the more the phone dinged, the more irritated Cole became.

It was the respect issue. The trait that Cole held above all.

Mariah had seemed like a woman who told the truth no matter what. Over the past few weeks, he had learned the woman had no tact. She just said her mind, and he adored that. How many people were that open and honest?

Not many. That Cole knew well enough.

So, what was she hiding with her phone that she kept slamming into the couch?

After the film ended, he helped her clean up the popcorn, and from the corner of his eye he caught the phone flash again. The screen lit up briefly, and he had to blink several times to clear his vision. Surely, he had to be misreading that number.

Forty-seven text messages? Just tonight?

Cole was rooted to his spot by the couch, popcorn bowl in hand.

Forty-seven?

That was more than a few messages. That was . . .

That was something else.

And he couldn't wrap his brain around it. That number, those texts, hit him like a punch to the chest, and all the air went out of his lungs. His reaction was raw, without justification, but he had it all the same. He should ask her about it, but for some reason he couldn't.

He didn't understand his own reaction.

A light hand pressed against his lower back, and Mariah reached around him, grabbing her phone from its resting place on the arm of the couch.

"Hey, are you joining me in the kitchen?" she asked.

Cole could only stare at her. She took the bowl from his hands.

What was she lying about? He wanted to ask – he truly did. The words reached his tongue but wouldn't move past his lips.

"No," he answered in a tight voice. "No, I think I need to go."

Mariah set the bowl on the counter and placed a hand at her waist. Her eyes narrowed and the intent behind that look was obvious. Cole might find her to be so incredibly sexy, especially when she wore those fitted leggings, but she was also a brilliantly educated woman. Studying was her strong suit.

"Wait. What is it? You were fine earlier. What changed your mind?"

"I'm not feeling too well, all of the sudden. I should go."

Cole had to shift his gaze. He should say something, give her an indication of what was bothering him. In a way, he was lying to her — a lie of omission — just as he believed she was lying to him. Hypocrisy at its finest. Yet, with her shrewd eyes examining him in that intense way she had about her, he had a sinking sensation that his little hedging lie was just as bad, if not worse, than whatever she might be hiding in those texts.

His body shook under his skin, and it took all his will power not to shove those somber thoughts to the side and wrap her luscious, welcoming body in his arms. Even now, trying not to look at her, his body responded, throbbing with the mere prospect of touching her.

Never had anyone affected him this way. He should just say something, anything, so they might end up in bed together, skin on skin, sharing their breathing and their bodies.

Instead, Cole took the low road and said nothing.

What was he doing? He preached openness and honesty and respect.

And here he was ducking out. All because he couldn't bring himself to talk about those texts.

"If something is wrong, you should tell me. Are you sick? Is there a problem?"

He couldn't argue with her logic, so he didn't. And it took all of his strength to not let his eyes flick over at her phone.

"I can't be here anymore. It's better if I leave."

Mariah's eyes narrowed as she crossed her arms over her full breasts. Her entire body hardened like stone.

"You aren't sick. I did something or said something, and now you're pissed. And you aren't going to tell me why?"

Cole didn't answer and grabbed his keys from the rickety table in the entryway. He didn't look at her. If he did, he would break. And right now, he thought it prudent to leave before he said something he might regret.

"What about all your claims of respect and honesty? Was that just a load of shit, Cole? If you respected me, you would sit down and talk to me, no matter how hard it is to say what's on your mind."

"I'll call you later," he said, regretting the words as they left his lips.

He gazed at her in a hooded side view for the space of three heartbeats. The hurt, stricken expression on her face told him she well understood the harshness behind his good-bye. She was still recovering from her ex, and here Cole was, being deceptive and breaking her heart again.

Nevertheless, he set his jaw and walked out the door.

And he regretted his decision to walk away all the more — so much so that by the time Cole headed home, he was on the phone, trying to call her. And at his core, he couldn't understand why he reacted in such a visceral way.

Each call went right to voice mail. And each text went unanswered.

Of course, they did. She was pissed at him for leaving so abruptly with no apparent reason.

He *had* a reason, at least in his opinion, but right now his reason seemed trivial and didn't matter for shit. Once he cooled off from his irate response to her cell phone, Cole had a fundamental realization. He'd made a stupid, gross assumption.

He'd screwed up.

For a man who prided himself on his strict control and tempered personality — God knew he needed it with some of his players — his irrational behavior tonight was shocking and foolish. *What the hell?* What was wrong with him?

He had asked, no — not really, demanded — respect, and when it came time for him to show his respect for Mariah, he trampled all over it like a seventh inning base hit run.

Because he got mad.

He'd thrown a fit.

UGH.

A screeching horn blared next to him, and Cole jerked to refocus his eyes on the dark road and yanked on the steering wheel. He'd drifted out of his lane. Lifting his foot off the gas pedal, he glanced down at his speedometer.

Shit. Over sixty? Cole slowed to a stop and pulled over, putting the car in park by the curb. Good thing no cops were around. The speed limit on Pine Street was forty. That would have been an expensive ticket.

He breathed in and out in a six-second count to calm his palpating chest and fast breathing. He was also lucky he didn't hyperventilate.

Once he was under control, he finished his drive to his unassuming two-bedroom condo and started dialing Mariah's number on repeat.

No answer.

He tried texting.

No response.

Tavi followed Cole into his bedroom, the fluffy retriever seeming to know something was wrong. Cole flung his shirt off and threw it on the bed. He gritted his teeth at the subtle irony of his anger at her ex's excessive texts when he was now doing the exact same thing.

He finished stripping down and donned a pair of loose sweats to sleep in but sleep never came. He petted Tavi's dozing head and stared at the ceiling.

One question kept rolling around in his mind.

Why had he reacted that way?

The pressure in his chest had intensified with each text from her ex, each vibration on her phone, built and built until he thought he'd explode.

And the whole time, his brain was latching on the overly-macho phrase "That's mine!"

Cole sat up in bed, his hyperventilating returning with a vengeance.

That was it. That was why he reacted so poorly. Shit, it had been a while for him — no wonder he didn't recognize it.

Mariah wasn't just a woman he was dating. She wasn't a one-night stand or a fling. He was building something with her, and when her ex overstepped, he wanted to pound the man into the ground.

Because Cole wanted to protect her. To care for her. To be a part of her life.

Because he loved her.

Chapter Nine

FRIDAY — AND AS much as Cole wanted to just go to the nearest dive bar and get shit-faced drunk, he had a long day at the athletic office scheduled and one of the last games of the regular season.

Fuck.

Though he tried to focus, nothing registered. He was on autopilot. He pulled it off during the day in the office, but his attention was noticeably absent before the game. Ken asked him three times about the lineup and what inning he was pitching. And his pre-game pep talk . . . He just recycled what he'd said the week before. His assistant coach, Jason Alzugaray, who usually preferred to stay in the background, picked up the rest of the pep talk with references to this final game of their regular season. Thank God for the assistant coach.

Cole zoned out for the first inning, and his players were suffering for it. Later in the game, though, Cole got his act together enough to keep his team on their toes, and they pulled a win at 6-5. Cole flushed with a hateful heat. He was pissed at the game and at himself. The Knights were a small college not known for their athletics, and the Hawks squeaked by with a one run lead?

What in the hell?

Cole kicked at the dirt on the field before heading toward the locker room. He knew who to blame for this gift win — himself. He let his emotions take hold and distract him, something he never did, and it could have cost them this important game. Playoffs started the following week. He couldn't risk another chancy game.

Now the angry heat at his core flared for two reasons, and the agonizing burden was becoming a vicious circle.

Running his hand through his thick hair, Cole replaced his blue cap and joined his team.

Time to face the music.

The players, however, didn't seem to notice. Or if they did, they didn't care. They laughed and clapped each other's backs in congratulations.

WHAT THE HELL?
They were proud of this pathetic win?

Charming

The world wasn't making sense. Cole's mind spun like he must have stumbled down a rabbit hole.

"Hey, Coach, close game but we pulled it off in the end there, didn't we?" Ken Xiao called out, his face bright with victory.

Cole's shoulders drooped. Even when he was at his worst, his players and his team rallied. His chest puffed with pride, and he stood a bit straighter.

"Yeah, you guys did it. Touch and go for a while in the fifth, but that last run in the ninth made our day. Next week, playoffs!"

The entire team's cheered echoed off the lockers, vibrating against the metal and drowning out every other sound. Cole waved his hands over his head to get their attention.

"To prepare for next week, Coach Alzugaray and I will review highlights from the Eagle's previous games and develop our strategy. I know next week is finals, but we will have an extra practice late Tuesday afternoon, until about eight. Are you ready to attack, Hawks?

"Yes, Coach!" Another echo from their unanimous accolades of victory.

At least his team hadn't noticed how distracted he'd been.

Cole hid in his office just off the locker rooms, door closed and phone out on his desk. He sunk into his decaying office chair, tossed his cap next to a stack of folders, and checked his phone again. Still nothing.

God damn.

Charming

A short knock on his door. Cole flinched, setting his phone on his desk and grabbing a paper to appear busy.

"Enter!"

Tannis's baby blues peered around the edge of the door.

"Hey, Coach, got a minute?"

Cole dropped the phony paper onto the desk and motioned to the metal chair across from him.

"What's up, Reyes?"

Tannis sat in the chair and pressed his palms into his knees. His normal, lopsided grin was absent from his face, and Cole stiffened. Tannis was here for something serious. More serious than the game they'd just won.

"So, I know you and Prof L are, like, a thing. You may be trying to keep it a secret, but it's a horribly kept one. FYI. People have seen you two together, in case you thought you were being discreet or whatever. The past weeks, man, you have been so happy. It's crazy, but I dunno. It's a good thing, Ok?"

Cole's chair squeaked as he leaned back and folded his hands on his chest. "Ok."

Tannis's eyes flicked around the room. "Today you seem really off. I mean really, Coach. Just not you. Unless your dog had a bad accident last night . . . ?"

Tannis trailed off and cast an expectant look at Coach, who shook his head from one side to the other while keeping his eyes on Tannis.

Tannis dropped his head. "Ok, so I know it's not my business . . ."

"It's not." Cole's voice was tight.

"But if something happened between you and Prof L," Tannis continued as if Cole hadn't spoken, "then you need to talk to her. Because it's affecting you. No offense, Coach," Tannis added quickly.

"Why are you telling me this, Tannis? Since when is my private life open to you?" Cole's words were more curt than he intended. Just another casualty of his self-inflicted ire.

"It's not, and I get that. But you are all about respect, Coach. And I dunno. I guess if I had a problem like that, one where it might affect my work or attention or whatever, I'd want someone to talk to me about it. You are always telling us to have each other's back, to treat our teammates and peers with respect. While you aren't exactly a teammate, you are still on my team, like the foundation of it. I would feel like I was disrespecting you if I didn't make sure everything was Ok."

Cole sucked on his lower lip.

Freakin' kid. Tannis was smarter than he gave himself credit for. Cole's gaze finally moved from Tannis to the office door. Tannis's words resonated deeper than the young man knew. That was what bothered Cole the most. He felt the excess texts and Mariah's offhand explanation showed a lack of respect, but his reaction to her was worse. She at least tried to give him a reason. He had left wordlessly.

And I have to practice what I preach.

"You're right, Tannis. I behaved in a way that doesn't align with what I lecture you guys about, and it bit me hard. I'm trying to figure out what to do next." *Because I may have blown it completely.*

"Maybe you need to give her the chance to explain. I mean, you always teach us about respect, and to me, if you respected her, you would ask her. You tell her why you did or said or whatever, and then listen to her explanation. I mean, it's not that hard, is it?"

Cole cut his eyes to Tannis in a sidelong gaze. *God damn kids, listening to his speeches.*

"No, no, it's not that hard, Reyes."

Tannis stood up. His cheeks pinked in a flush — a mixture of sun, excitement from the game, and anxiety over talking man-to-man with his coach — and he brushed at the reddish dust on his once-white uniform pants as he walked to the door.

"We good, Coach?" he asked as he opened the door. "I didn't overstep, did I?"

Cole shook his head again. "No, Reyes. You're fine. Thank you for taking the time to talk to me."

Tannis's cheeks pulled into a flashy smile — there it was. His infamous smile was back.

"Anytime, Coach."

Then he slammed the door behind him.

Well, the kid had learned something, if not how to close a door.

By the time Cole reached his car, he'd left too many messages and voice mails to count. No response, so it was time to take decisive action. He hadn't changed or showered, and a layer of dirt and field dust clung to him.

He stopped at a floral shop — probably the last one in existence – that was tucked into a corner of a dumpy shopping center. Cole thought all floral shops closed and was actually considering going to the grocery store for whatever leftover flowers they had when he saw the open sign.

Who still bought flowers at a flower shop?

Cole realized the irony of his thought when the door jingled as he entered. *He* bought flowers at a flower shop.

A white-haired lady came up to him as he tried to take in the multi-chromatic assault on his senses.

"How bad?" she asked in a flat voice.

Cole swiveled around and looked down at her. Her sour face didn't hide her knowing expression.

"What?"

"How bad? How bad did you screw up? Is it a half-dozen roses bad? Or a dozen roses paired with hydrangeas and a card? How bad?"

Christ, the woman's terrific at her job. Maybe that was why this store was still in existence.

"The dozen with the two other things you said."

"That bad, eh? Well, come to the counter then. You can fill out the card while I get your blooms together. Might I recommend the blue and green card with the birds?"

She waggled her fingers to the counter set midway through the store, and Cole grabbed the card she recommended. It was blank on the inside.

Great. I don't even know what to write.

Charming

"Just write 'I'm sorry' and your name!" the white-haired lady's voice cackled from behind a mountain of flower displays.

Cole did as she commanded, and then hesitated with what to write before his name. *Love? Yours? Truly?* He wasn't Shakespeare.

"If you love her, 'Love' is fine," the wizened voice called again.

Cole now understood why this woman's store was in business. She was like an oracle or something.

An exquisite-looking display shelf next to him caught his attention. The woman's lips curled into a grin as he grabbed one of the items from the shelf and added it to his flowers.

The woman's knowing gaze never left him as she rang up his order. He clutched his apology gifts the way a drowning man seizes a life jacket and raced for the door.

"Good luck!" she called out just before the door closed behind him.

He didn't call Mariah again. It was getting dark, and if he recalled her schedule well enough, then she should be at home, grading essays and getting ready for finals.

A knock on the door, flowers and card in front of him, and a contrite expression on his face.

That was what she would see when she opened the door. *If* she opened the door.

To say he was shocked when she did appear at the doorway, though she opened it with obvious begrudging effort, would be an understatement. She was long and lean in a floor length skirt and a fitted top. Her wavy hair fell loose around her face where the clip didn't keep it contained.

"Thank you," he started, and she invited him in, then closed the door behind him.

So far so good.

Then she spoke, a harsh biting tone that put Cole in his place. "Do you think flowers will make up for how you spoke to me, treated me, last night?"

Everything about her was hard, angry. And he couldn't blame her in the least.

"There's also a card," Cole offered weakly.

He thrust the flowers and card into her hands. Mariah exhaled fiercely through her nose but accepted the gifts and took the flowers to the kitchen.

"Read the card, Ok?"

The glance she flashed him would have cut ice. A light sweat sprouted on his forehead as he waited with excruciating patience for her to open the card.

"I know you're sorry," Mariah said, flapping the card at him. She didn't appear moved. *Maybe the old flower lady was wrong?*

"I have one more gift. Just promise me you won't break it because you're mad at me."

Her stern expression didn't change. Cole pulled his hand out from behind his back. A scalloped teacup painted with delicate blue and purple flowers and edged with green and gold leaf filigree sat in the center of his palm.

"To replace the one that broke. I hope this is what you were talking about. I don't know one teacup from the next."

Her expression finally shifted, softening, and her eyes widened. She reached for the cup, then gently set it on the counter next to the flowers. Her eyes studied it for several seconds as her fingers traced the curved edges. Then she turned around to face Cole.

That, he thought, *might be progress.*

"Please, let me explain," he started.

She dropped the card onto the counter with the other gifts, then leaned her back against the counter's edge. She waved a hand at him. Her face showed nothing.

"Go ahead."

"I didn't know what was going on, and I made a bad assumption. I didn't realize that this thing with your ex was a problem, nothing more. I wish you would have said something to me before this all got out of hand. How can I take care of you—"

"I don't need someone to take care of me! I'm a grown ass woman, and I can handle some off the wall ex. I didn't want to drag you into drama like that or for you to think you needed to take care of me."

"But I could have helped you —" he started.

"That's not the point!" Her voice hit a pitch, and she placed her hand on the table for a moment, struggling to find some modicum of inner peace. She cleared her throat and calmed her voice.

"I don't want you to think you have to take care of me. That I can't do it myself. I needed to deal with Derek myself, not drag you through that muck. I thought he'd stop soon enough. The fact he didn't made all this —" she waved her hand around her head, "so much more difficult."

Cole stilled with his hands clenched by his side. Her explanation made complete, logical sense, and he had blamed her for supposedly hiding something from him.

I'm such a jerk. It was a difficult admission to make.

Mariah cleared her throat again. "I'm sorry I hid it—"

"No," Cole interrupted her, dropping his chin to his chest. "No, you don't need to apologize. I do."

"Cole—"

"No, hear me out, please." He gave Mariah a slow nod. "You had every right to keep that under wraps. You didn't know it would get out of control like that, and I do appreciate that you didn't want that guy's shit to rub off on me."

Cole reached out his hand, taking a risk to touch Mariah's hand that was still planted on the table.

"I'm sorry that I made a bad assumption. I'm sorry that when I did ask, and asked badly, I didn't give you the opportunity to explain. I'm a coach, you're the writer. I have a bit to learn about communication from you, I think."

His humbled tone was too much for Mariah, and she blinked back tears. She had truly relished Cole's love and attention, and when she thought she'd lost it, a crushing dread had filled her. Her red-rimmed eyes told their own story.

"We can both learn a bit about communication. I promise that, in the future if I'm struggling with something, I'll let you know. Even if I don't need or want your help, but just so you know. And if I do need your help, I will ask for it."

Cole stepped around the table and clasped her slender hand in his so their palms touched. His touch was electric.

"And I won't make assumptions about you again. I know you are an empowered woman, and as your boyfriend, it's easy for me to forget that. I have this deep desire to take care of you, but out of respect, I will only step in if you ask."

He moved closer and the musky scent of his body spray and his male pheromones made her senses whirl.

"That is," he continued, "if I am still your boyfriend?"

He sounds like a nervous middle schooler! She pinched her mouth tight, but a wisp of a smile curled her lips. Cole was so sincere — how could she turn that away?

I can't.

Mariah dropped his hands and wrapped her arms around his neck.

"Yes, you're still my boyfriend."

Cole bent his head, and their lips met in a heated, apologetic kiss. Cole shifted, tugging his lips away.

"Wait. Was this our first fight?"

Mariah's eyes crinkled as she nodded.

"Yes, I believe it was."

"Does that mean we get to have make up sex?"

Again, with the middle school tone!

"Yes, I think —"

Before she could finish, Cole lifted Mariah under her arms, and she squeaked at the surprise. He set her so she was sitting on the table's edge as he stood between her legs.

"No, this was mostly my fault. I think I need to make it up to you."

"Cole, what—?"

Charming

His brawny hands flipped up the edge of her maxi-length skirt, his fingers dancing their way to her narrow thatch of hair between her thighs.

"I think I need to *really* apologize."

The sultry expression on his face gave away his intentions, and Mariah let her legs fall open.

"Well, if you insist."

Cole grinned wickedly and popped his head under her skirt so her view of him was his backside before it disappeared under the black fabric. Her panties pulled taut against her hips as he pushed them to the side, so he had full access.

His mouth breathed warm puffs on her lower lips, followed by the light whip of his tongue. Up and down, over and across before flicking against her nerve bud, first slow then picking up speed.

He brought her to the brink until her hand clawed at him under the thin layer of her skirt, then his tongue withdrew, and then started again.

"Please," she begged, panting as she gripped his shoulder, the table, anything to stop her from falling. The whole world was spinning, and she was slipping off the edge of it.

"Are you sure?" he asked in a muffled voice.

Mariah threw her head back as he resumed his pattern, then his lips wrapped around her clit and a shock of electric ecstasy washed over her in wave after wave. She screeched as she came, wetting his chin with her sweet juices.

Cole's handsomely dark head reappeared from under her skirt, his chin and lips glistening before he slowly wiped his face with the side of his hand. He then rubbed his lips with his index and middle finger in the sexiest single languid movement. Mariah's breathing quickened again at the seductive gesture, knowing he was wiping her wetness from his lips.

Mariah thought her chest would explode. Then he leaned over her, placing his palms on either side of her hips so his wet mouth was centimeters from hers.

"Want a taste?" his rumbling voice asked.

She didn't answer. She pressed upward to catch his lips and share in what he offered.

Cole leaned back again, this time with a slightly abashed look on his face. He lifted his hand to played with her riotous curls, wrapping locks that had escaped her clip around each of his fingers.

"I love your curls." His breath was warm against her damp skin.

"Really? I think they are annoying," she said in a seductive tone.

"They are like an extension of everything you are, wild and brilliant and unexpected."

His closeness, his raspy voice, the strangely sweet smell of her nectar on him — it was all an impossible, heady moment. A piece of time that had paused, and only the two of them floated in the universe.

Mariah laid her hand on his cheek, not wanting to break the powerful stillness. She'd caught his meaning — what he was trying to say with his tender words.

"The curls are me?"

He dipped his head briefly before raising his shimmering, amber eyes to her. Her breath caught in her lungs,

100

and she knew she'd not be able to start breathing again until she heard what he was trying to say.

"I love you, Mariah. And I was so afraid I almost lost you."

She shifted her face to his, kissing his top lip, then his bottom lip before moving to his ear.

"That's why it all hurt so bad. I love you, Cole."

It was the teacup that did it. He'd remembered when she had cried over her broken one. That little porcelain cup told her more about Cole and how he felt than any words he might speak. And her reaction to it spoke volumes about her feelings toward him. He had entwined himself into her heart, something Mariah had not expected, so hard and so sudden, and she was still trying to work through her emotions. Which had made ignoring all of Cole's texts and calls more difficult. But she didn't want to risk saying anything she might regret. Waiting a day gave her time to cool down.

Their first spat in the books, and they were stronger than before, if such a thing were possible. And since they made it through that, and Cole had told her about his conversation with Tannis, they decided that it was time to make it official. Not only did that mean Mariah finally got to meet the adorably rambunctious Tavi, but it also meant dealing with the fallout on campus.

Charming

Campus gossip had been growing terribly rife over the past week, and both Cole and Mariah had to have a sit-down with HR. That was one of the most uncomfortable conversations she'd ever had — even worse than the apology session between herself and Cole.

The assistant director of Human Resources, Joan Reed, ushered them through the door and gestured to two padded office chairs in front of her desk. Her salt-and-pepper hair was pulled back into a tight bun that Mariah admired. *How did she get her hair so smooth?* she thought in a momentary distraction.

Joan tapped a short stack of papers on her desk.

"First, let me say I appreciate that you came to me right away. You can't imagine how many times faculty or staff date, then break up, and then it becomes an HR nightmare."

Cole and Mariah both tittered uncomfortably.

Slipping a pair of blue readers onto her nose, Joan looked over the paperwork before she slid the papers to Cole and Mariah.

"The good news is there is a bit of an academic wall between you two. Different departments, different supervisors, and it's not a superior/subordinate relationship. All those things work in your favor. As long as you remain professional on campus, you aren't *technically* breaking any campus rules. These packets are just the MLC policy on campus relationships. Go and live happily."

Joan waved them off, and Cole and Mariah grabbed their packets and exited the office. Mariah leaned against the shaded building wall once they were outside.

Charming

The HR rep put a strange emphasis on the word "technically," and Mariah had the idea that there were some rules they were skirting on, but HR couldn't enforce them, so they were willing to look the other way.

"That went better than I thought it would," Cole admitted. Mariah had to agree.

"Too bad we had the HR meeting just now. Otherwise, I could kiss you before you leave for the athletic fields."

A twinkle shimmered in Cole's eyes, and his fingers brushed her hand. "Maybe I can sneak a kiss after class one day."

Mariah peered up at Cole from under hooded eyes. "Oh, you are saying this right after our HR meeting? You're a bad boy."

"I never claimed otherwise. So, that's a yes?"

Mariah's fingers responded to Cole's touch, tracing along his knuckles.

"Surprise me. That way at least one of us has deniability."

Cole looked to the left and right, then stepped a breath closer to Mariah.

"Look at you, always thinking,"

The sound of student chatter broke their private moment. Cole shifted backwards and stiffened. Mariah burst into a laugh at his sheepish expression.

"I know you have a late class tonight. How about I meet you after and walk you to your car?" he asked.

"I'd like that. We're usually done by ten."

Cole flicked his head back and forth once more, and seeing the students had turned the corner, he risked a quick kiss

103

on her cheek. Then he spun around, flashed her a stunning smile over his shoulder, and headed toward the baseball field.

Mariah didn't know how Cole's players reacted to the rumors, but her students were a bit ruthless when the news officially broke. Tannis used every opportunity to make subtle, suggestive comments, or worse, overt statements about Coach. Try as she might, Mariah couldn't stop the blush that rose to her cheeks when Tannis was on a roll. The kid was a class clown extraordinaire.

After class on Tuesday, Tannis came up to her desk. Classes were ending after finals the following week, and she knew Tannis was worried about his grade. It was the one time this semester she'd seem him worried about anything. He'd done better on the previous essay, due to his help from his tutor, and garnered a high "C" of which he was pretty proud. But the final essay was worth twice as much and involved more work than the previous one. At first, Mariah thought he was coming up to her to talk about his upcoming final essay. Instead, Tannis surprised her.

"I'm sorry about all that, Professor L. The jokes in class and all. You just have to understand. Like, we've never seen Coach date before. I mean, I know he's had to have girlfriends before and stuff, but *we've* never met them. You, it's great because you're right here, and we all know you."

Oh, yes. Great.

Mariah tipped her chin at him. "Um, that's good to know, I guess?"

A wide smile split Tannis's tanned face. "Professor L, it's all good. The whole team likes you. If you ever need anything, or if Coach isn't giving you enough attention, just let me know. He can get wrapped up in his team way too much."

Mariah blinked rapidly as a fevered blush warmed her cheeks. *What am I supposed to say to that?*

"Um, thanks?"

Tannis winked at her. "Have a good day, Professor L."

Then he sauntered off, the way cocky, confident athletes tend to do. It was the same walk she'd seen on Cole after they won a game.

Charming

Chapter Ten

IT TOOK A COUPLE of days for the gossip about their relationship to die down — of course it would, Mariah knew. Still, she was grateful that her relationship with Cole was no longer the subject of gossip for the students and staff. The whole situation made her feel like she was back in high school, of all things.

Especially since Cole relished in walking her to and from class, carrying her books no less. Honestly, how had he been here on campus all this time and she'd never noticed?

Charming

Her Thursday night class ended early and all her students were stressed as finals neared. They appreciated getting out a few minutes ahead of schedule and scrambled for the door. Mariah took her time organizing her papers and looking over the final essays that had been submitted. The stack on her desk looked too tall, and final essays meant the start of a long weekend with refills of tea and time on the couch with her red pen. She had already let Cole know that she was out of commission this weekend.

Which worked well for him — he had to leave early Friday afternoon on what he called "the stink bus" for the playoff game against the Occidental Tigers, and he wouldn't return until late. Then Saturday would be review day for the team. Cole promised to stop by on Sunday to say hi, if she were far enough along in her grading.

Oh, the trials of college life, she joked to herself as she counted the papers in the stack. *Twenty-two. Not bad.* That meant every student at least turned in something. Whether it was a full essay or not remained to be seen.

The classroom door creaked open as she finished tucking the essays in her bag.

"Cole," she said, not looking up. "I've got twenty-two papers from this class. I'm glad I got a head start on grading for my other classes last night."

"Who the fuck is Cole?"

Mariah froze with her hand still in her bag and her head down.

She knew that voice, and she'd grown to loathe anything related to it. That *the-world-owes-me-something* voice made the hairs on the back of her neck rise.

Zipping her bag closed, she stood upright and glared at the blond nightmare lounging against the door.

"Really, Derek? You can't be bothered to meet me on campus in the months I dated you. Now that I've blocked you, you decide to come? I don't think so. Get out now. Don't make me call campus police."

"I don't think you'll do that. You're not the type," Derek drawled as he sauntered past the desks, dragging a long finger across the surfaces.

Leisurely, like he had all the time in the world. With her jaw clenched tight, Mariah threw her bag over her shoulder and tilted her head at Derek.

"Then you don't know me as well as you thought. I'm done with you, Derek. Done. I blocked you on my phone and social media. Any trace of you in my life has been tossed in the trash. You can't come here and try to win me back, or whatever the hell this is." She started to walk past the instructor's desk, moving for the door. "Now, it's time for me to leave. I have papers to grade. Get out. And don't come back."

"Oh, papers," he jeered in a strange falsetto. He threw his hands up to wave them as he spoke, and before she could walk past him, Derek grabbed the strap of her bag. Mariah pulled at his hand, trying unsuccessfully to release his grip. Her heart leapt to her throat.

Charming

"What the hell, Derek?"

"Yeah. What the hell, Derek?" a deep, angry voice called from the doorway.

Mariah spun as far as she could with Derek still clutching her bag to find Cole filling the doorway to the classroom. A rush of relief flowed through Mariah. His build made Derek's lean physique seem almost frail. Had she forgotten just how muscular Cole was? In his blue sweats, made even darker by the night sky, he exuded constrained power.

But what drew her attention was his face. His handsome, dark features had transformed into something vicious, much like the hardened look he had on the field only more severe, a dreadful entity ready to wreak havoc. He'd been upset when he learned of Derek's harassing texts, but Mariah had never seen Cole truly furious. And right now, he appeared truly furious. And it was a frightening thing to see.

"Who the fuck are you?" Derek asked.

Mariah jerked away from Derek and moved in between the two men. She gave Cole a look that said *let me handle this.* He stiffened but didn't move from the door.

"Derek, this is my boyfriend. We're on our way out, and I need to lock this door. You need to go home and move on with your life."

Derek's inflamed eyes flicked to Cole and back to Mariah.

"Really? Just weeks after you dumped me, and you already have a boyfriend? What are you, some sort of whore?"

His face closed in on hers. Mariah didn't flinch. Knowing that Cole was standing right behind her gave Mariah a sense of bravado she hadn't expected in a confrontation like this. She stood her ground, nose to nose with Derek, and flapped her hand at fury-riddled Cole who stepped directly behind her.

"No, just a woman smart enough to get out of a bad relationship. I don't know what you want from someone Derek, but it's not me. This isn't about you, anymore. Get over it. Now leave."

Cole had moved near enough to Mariah that the heat of his rage burned against her back. That hot, constrained power of his.

Derek grabbed for her bag strap again, and over her shoulder, a thick, bronzed arm landed on Derek's wrist, gripping it so tightly that Derek's skin grew red.

"She said leave."

Cole's hard voice left no room for discussion.

Derek snatched his hand back and shoved forward, trying to launch himself at Cole. Which meant pushing at Mariah as well.

And that was a big mistake. Cole spun around as graceful as a dancer and put Derek in a headlock. Derek grunted and twisted, trying to break free, but Cole's arms flexed like steel bars against his neck. And Cole hadn't even broken a sweat. He raised his eyes to Mariah.

"Can I give you some help now?" he said it earnestly, not in an *I told you so* tone. Mariah nodded, speechless. Cole dropped his eyes back to the flailing Derek.

"Ok, bud, let me tell you what's gonna happen here. She said leave. You're going to leave. Don't bug her again, don't contact her. We're going to notify campus security and

111

the local police, and they will act if they see you near her or even set foot on this campus. Worse, if I hear you made any contact, text, phone, DM, fucking smoke signal, I will deal with you personally. And I promise you," Cole's voice dropped dangerously low, "you don't want that."

Releasing Derek with the same sudden movement as he had trapped him, Cole shifted to block Mariah from Derek's view. He crossed his arms over his chest, waiting to see what the man would do next.

Derek's eyes never left Cole, and he ran from the room like the devil himself was behind him. From the ferocious expression on Cole's face, maybe Derek was right to run.

"Like a cowardly dog," Cole said with a huff.

Mariah had the same thought — Derek reminded her of a dog with his tail between his legs.

Then all her energy left her, and she slumped against Cole's firm back. Cole swung around and gathered her in his arms. They stayed like that for a while, until Mariah finally found her voice.

"Can you take me home?" she asked.

"In a heartbeat."

Cole walked her to her car and followed her to her apartment, then joined her inside. Mariah's hair had escaped her clip and surrounded her head in waves of chaos, and her face was pinched. *Worry? Exasperation? Fear?* She seemed too anxious to be by herself. Not that Cole was about to leave her alone anyway, even though he was certain Derek was not coming back. Some guys were nothing but hot air, and Cole could identify a guy like that a mile away. Derek was gone for good.

"Will he come back? Be a bother? Do I need safety precautions in my apartment?"

Cole's embrace tightened. "No, I think you will be Ok. He knows that you now have connections to the police and campus security, both of which we need to contact either tonight or tomorrow first thing, by the way. And you have a fearsome boyfriend who doesn't mess around. Guys like him, they want easy prey. But he should have known, even without anyone else getting involved, you weren't easy prey."

Mariah rested her forehead against his chest, inhaling his scent of post-practice dust and musk.

"Maybe we need to realize it's not just you or me, it's us. And you can handle anything," Cole spoke into her hair. "I'm sure, but if you need to tag someone in, I will always have your back. But the thing is, Mariah, you don't have to handle everything. I'd like to carry some of that weight for you, just like you carry some of mine, even if you don't know it. And if that weight is dealing with a messed-up ex, so be it. I'll carry it gladly."

"You need to know he doesn't haunt me anymore," Mariah told him, tracing the outline of a pectoral muscle with her finger. "I lost interest in him the day I kicked him out. I deserve better and I got it — with you. And we can carry any weight together."

Cole knew this was the type of relationship he always craved — one with a woman who knew what she wanted and respected what he wanted as well. Communication, mutual respect, that was sexy as hell. And hot looks to go with it all? Cole promised himself he wasn't about to lose that.

"Want me to stay the night?"

She placed a bent finger under her chin and stared at him as if she were studying a student.

"I want you to stay forever."

Several pounding heartbeats passed as they held each other's gaze. Was she asking to move in together?

"Does this mean what I think it means?" he asked.

She gave him one slow blink. "Yes."

This, *this* was what he wanted — to spend the rest of his life with this loud, brash, passionate woman.

"My place is bigger, and I have my dog. He makes a great guard dog," Cole responded, then swept Mariah into his arms and carried her the short distance to her bedroom, their lips locked the whole way, sealing their future.

They could work out the details later.

The End

Enjoy this sweet and sexy romance? Want to read more hot campus romances? Check out all the books in the Campus Heat Series, and take a peek at book 2: *Tempting*.

Excerpt from Tempting

SABRINA WALKED INTO the writing center in a flustered huff. Today had started so well, especially after the past few weeks!

Her old-fashioned, "You aren't one of those empowered females" type boyfriend was finally done. She had almost slapped him when he said he believed women were supposed to be submissive.

What the hell? Was he stuck in the 1950s? She wasn't looking for a Mrs. Degree at MLC!

116

Evan just didn't get it. And he wasn't worth the air it took to explain it to him.

Who today thinks he can get away with that? Not with Sabrina Alonto. That's for certain.

They had broken up a while ago, and he'd tried a few times to hook up with her and had only gotten the hint after she blocked his number. Now he was done, gone, and for the past several weeks, life had improved significantly. Even today, a bright and sunny Southern California day, mirrored her exuberance as she got out of bed.

She had been feeling good, dammit! She was getting As in all her classes, including professor Antez's stats class. The semester was almost over – finals were next week, so all she had to do was hang on until then. And to make sure she could still work at the writing center over summer, she enrolled in the impacted Soc 200 course and got in! Everything was going so well!

Then, just as things were looking up, they all slammed back down. It was like the universe saved up all its karma and unloaded it on her before noon.

First, her roommate Diana said she couldn't afford to stay in the apartment over the summer. *What the hell?* How was Sabrina supposed to pay for the rent alone? And there was no way she'd find a roommate who needed a three-month lease over the summer.

Fuckery number 1.

Then her computer ate her English paper. She was almost done, and she had her previous saved version, but all her revisions were gone. *Gone*! It was due tomorrow, so now she'd have to pull an all-nighter after her shift at the writing center to get it done.

Fuckery number 2.

And she almost didn't make it to campus anyway – her car stalled twice before turning over, and Sabrina had no idea what was going on. The car wasn't even that old, and she'd taken it in for an oil change last month. Once she was parked on campus, she dialed the local repair shop, and they said they could get her in tomorrow.

And there was Fuckery number 3.

Sabrina's mind was on her car and how she hoped it started when it was time to leave the writing center, and she didn't notice her two o'clock appointment waiting by the small conference room door in the library.

"Tannis! I'm sorry. Am I late?"

Sabrina juggled her backpack and her purse, trying to check the time. Clocking in late would be the cherry on top of this miserable day.

"No, no. Class got out early, so you're all good. Don't apologize."

He gave her one of his winning smiles, a smile straight from a toothpaste commercial. That, with his cinnamon-blond hair, sky-blue eyes, and his athletic physique, it was no wonder he was one of the most sought-after guys on campus. Either as a friend or to date.

And it probably fed the rumors that he was a thirst trap and a player.

The thirst trap she could understand. Too often she found herself daydreaming about him after their tutoring sessions, wondering if that amber sprinkle of freckles appeared elsewhere on his body.

But as a player? Sabrina didn't have time for that. Plus, she wasn't the popular, go-to-all-the-games-and-parties type, so she wasn't *his* type.

Popular baseball players didn't go for the smart girls.

She still admired his handsome body and the relaxed way he held himself. Christ, he didn't have a care in the world.

Must be nice.

Sabrina took a deep breath and flashed a tight smile to Tannis.

"Ok, then why don't you grab a seat and get your paper, and I'll join you as soon as I clock in."

With that smile, Tannis could melt butter. A panty dropper for sure.

"Sure thing, boss!"

Oh, to have such a nonchalant attitude, not a worry in the world like that lovely man.

After her morning, she wasn't sure she could handle his positivity. It was almost too much. She sighed. It wouldn't be the first time she wore a fake smile for the day.

"Ok, so here is what you need to fix. Remember when Professor L said you need to have more than one sentence for your intro and your conclusion?"

Tannis studied the paper on the table and bit his lip. No, he didn't remember. Was his thesis sentence in the introduction? What else did it need?

"I guess I don't remember that. What do I need to put in the intro? Or the conclusion?"

Sabrina tried not to let her aggravation show on her face as she grabbed her info sheet from her backpack. How did teachers deal with students like this? She had a newfound respect for her professors and vowed she would never become one.

Tannis's eyes remained on his paper. Writing had never been his strong suit. So many rules, so many ways to get it right or do it wrong. Sabrina placed a colorful sheet on the table.

"See here?" She pointed with a chipped nail polished finger. "This shows some of the things you can add to craft your introduction. Do any of these look like they might work?"

Tannis reviewed the sheet, picked ideas to add to his introduction and conclusion, and made notes on his paper. Sabrina remembered all these little rules, wrote papers that met the page requirements, and made it look so simple.

"Ok, Tannis, we're just about done. Any more questions?"

Look at her, sitting across from him with an air of confidence. I bet she doesn't have to worry about failing any of her classes and losing her scholarship. Tannis bit his lip, afraid of her answer to his question.

"Do you think it's good enough to get a C? Or even a B? Lenski can be a tough grader."

"Yeah, but only on certain things. As long as you are nailing those, you can do pretty well in her class."

Tannis's chest burned. "Did I nail any of those things?" He hated the hesitance in his voice, and Professor L was a great teacher, but his anxiety was real. Tannis needed to pass this class.

"Fixing the intro and conclusion will help. Are you worried about your grade? You've met with me for two other essays, and you said you did Ok on those. I would think that means you can get a C in the class, easy."

Slouching in his metal chair, Tannis huffed out a sarcastic laugh. "Yeah, you'd think so. But I've missed some homework, and I tanked that first paper. It's why she recommended I come here."

Sabrina's wise, sable eyes scrutinized him like he was under a microscope as she leaned forward on the table. "You can always take the class again, if you fail."

Tannis shook his head. "Doesn't work that way. I have a baseball scholarship. Not a huge one, but it makes up the difference for what I can't pay for college. If I lose that, I'm not playing ball anymore, mostly because I won't be here."

She leaned forward even more, her attentive eyes mesmerizing. Sabrina had a way of looking at someone as though they were the only person in the room. And right now, that intense gaze on was on him. His bravado slipped under that gaze.

Check out Tempting by M.D. Dalrymple!

Want to read more from M.D. Dalrymple? Want to read some hot police romance? Check out all her books in the Men in Uniform series. Take a peek at an excerpt from book one: *Night Shift*

Excerpt from Night Shift

If you like Campus Romances by M.D Dalrymple, you'll also enjoy her police romances – The Men in Uniform Series. Take a peek at *Night Shift:*

MATTHEW RECALLED THE events from the night before, evaluating his behavior (wiping his hands on his running shorts in memory of the slimy film that covered the male offender — sometimes the sensation remained even after several showers), checking to make sure he acted by the book. As both offenders were healthy and booked into jail by early morning, Matthew and his brothers in blue considered that a win.

Charming

His mind on other matters, he paid little attention as he rounded a sharp curve of the trail. Just as he congratulated himself over a well-executed arrest, a huge German Shepherd ran onto the path, tethered by a long leash. Matthew twisted to the side of the trail to avoid tripping over the dumb beast. The animal emitted one loud bark, and Matthew paused give the dog's owner a dressing down. While he did admire the dog — the animal was a perfect specimen, it could have been a show dog — his mouth, ready to confront the owner, snapped shut.

At the other end of the tethered leash stood a slender, fairly tall woman, bright running shoes extending up to firm, tanned legs. His eyes traveled up her body, over her tiny running shorts that displayed her muscular thighs, over her fitted (*beautifully fitted,* he thought) tank top, to her angular face and sleek, ebony hair pulled back in a tight, low ponytail. Matthew's chest and loins clenched simultaneously, a sensation he had not experienced several years.

The woman reached her hand out to make sure he wasn't going to fall, and Matthew almost took it in his. Shaking his head to clear it, he snatched his hand back.

"You OK?" The woman's liquid voice asked. "Carter just rushed out. He's normally so obedient and stays by my side, but we haven't gone for a run in several days, and he was excited. I am so sorry."

Concern painted her face. She was rambling, and Matthew bit the inside of his lip to stop a grin.

"No, you are good. I was able to move around him. No blood, no foul."

This time Matthew smiled, and the enchanting woman before him returned the gesture in a radiant glow. Matthew fell into that smile and was lost. He didn't even know her name.

"Beautiful dog," he said, trying to keep her engaged. Her dark eyes sparkled with pride at the poor dog sitting obediently by her side. Carter kept looking down the trail and back at his mistress, probably wondering, *why aren't we running?*

"Oh, thanks," she replied, reaching to give her good boy a pat, and the dog pressed his head against her leg. The dog obviously loved her unconditionally. Matthew just met her and understood the dog's feelings. The electricity he felt from her burned deep within him.

"May I pet him?" Matthew reached forward and placed his hand at the dog's nose when the woman nodded. "Is he a purebred?"

Her silky hair shimmered as she nodded. "Yep, a gift from my parents when I moved out. They didn't want me living by myself."

"Good choice of a dog for that," Matthew told her. "One of my buddies is in the K9 Unit and cannot stop talking about how amazing the dog is. I've seen his shepherd in action more than once, and Germans are so well trained."

"You've seen a K9 in action? Are you a cop?"

Matthew's smile widened. He loved his job, even after asinine nights like the one before, and enjoyed telling people about it.

"Yeah, out of Tustin."

"Oh, do you live near here, then? Not Tustin? Running and all?" She gestured a slender hand at his running shorts. He had a flashing thought he hoped his package looked tempting.

"Yeah, just west of the park." He held out a hand, praying it wasn't too sweaty. He knew from experience how well *that* went over. "I'm Matthew, by the way."

"Oh, I'm Rosemarie."

Start the Men In Uniform romance series with Night Shift

And just as a reminder! If you love this book, be sure to leave a review! Reviews are life blood for authors, and I appreciate every review I receive!

Don't forget! If you want more from Michelle, go to the website to receive three FREE short ebooks, updates, and more in your inbox!

https://linktr.ee/mddalrympleauthor

A Note

As a college professor, and a former college and grad student, I have a wealth of information about college campus life at my disposal. And since I've been reading more professor-troped romances as of late, I thought to myself, *I have an inside view on this! Why am I not writing these romances for my readers?*

And *voila*! For this book I decided to start with something a bit different – a professor and another authority figure on campus: the coach. Have you seen some of these college ball coaches? YUM.

However, I have about seven or so books planned for the series, which will include all types of different campus relationship. And each will be a mix of sweet with a fine amount of steam!

I am so excited to begin this campus romance journey with you. Thank you for coming along for the ride!

I also have to thank all my college friends and colleagues throughout the years who've given me fodder for my writing.

And I want to thank my family and my hubby – my real-world HEA.

About the Author

Michelle Deerwester-Dalrymple is a professor of writing and an author. She started reading when she was 3 years old, writing when she was 4, and published her first poem at age 16. She has written articles and essays on a variety of topics, including several texts on writing for middle and high school students. She is also working on a novel inspired by actual events. She lives in California with her family of seven.

You can visit her blog page, sign up for her newsletter, and follow all her socials at:
https://linktr.ee/mddalrympleauthor

Charming

Also by the Author:

Glen Highland Romance

The Courtship of the Glen –Prequel Short Novella
To Dance in the Glen – Book 1
The Lady of the Glen – Book 2
The Exile of the Glen – Book 3
The Jewel of the Glen – Book 4
The Seduction of the Glen – Book 5
The Warrior of the Glen – Book 6
An Echo in the Glen – Book 7
The Blackguard of the Glen – Book 8 coming soon!

The Celtic Highland Maidens

The Maiden of the Storm
The Maiden of the Grove
The Maiden of the Celts – coming soon
The Maiden of the Loch – coming soon
The Maiden of the Stones – coming soon

Historical Fevered Series – short and steamy romance!

The Highlander's Scarred Heart
The Highlander's Legacy
The Highlander's Return
Her Knight's Second Chance
The Highlander's Vow
Her Knight's Christmas Gift

Charming
Her Outlaw Highlander

As M.D. Dalrymple - Men in Uniform

Night Shift – Book 1
Day Shift – Book 2
Overtime – Book 3
Holiday Pay – Book 4
School Resource Officer – book 5
Holdover – book 6 coming soon!

Campus Heat

Charming – Book 1
Tempting – Book 2
Infatuated – Book 3
Craving – Book 4

Printed in Great Britain
by Amazon